Soul of the Shoe

Douglas Knick

www.ten16press.com - Waukesha, WI

Soul of the Shoe
Copyrighted © 2024 by Douglas Knick

PB ISBN: 9781645385783
Edition 1

Soul of the Shoe
by Douglas Knick

Cover art by Julie Schweiss

All Rights Reserved. Written permission must be secured from the publisher to use or reproduce any part of this book, except for brief quotations in critical reviews or articles.

For information, please contact:

www.ten16press.com
Waukesha, WI

This book is a work of fiction. Names, characters, places, and incidents are the product of the author's imagination or are used fictitiously. Characters in this book have no relation to anyone bearing the same name and are not based on anyone known or unknown to the author. Any resemblance to actual businesses or companies, events, locales, or persons, living or dead, is coincidental.

*For all the students I have been blessed to walk beside,
those who shared with me a part of their soul*

"Cinderella is proof that a new pair of shoes can change your life."
~Author unknown

"My wish for you is that you continue. Continue. To be who and how you are, to astonish a mean world with your acts of kindness."
~Maya Angelou

Chapter 1

Work, it's such a distraction from life. A distraction from all the stuff I consider important.

It interrupts my sleep only to make me more tired. To yearn to return to the comforts of my bed. My bed actually isn't all that special or unique. I'd like to say it's an antique, worth a bucket of money, but it's not. It's just old. Old isn't antique. It's a hand-me-down. The twin bed, with a rusty metal frame concealed by the box spring, once belonged to my mother. When I graduated from the crib to a big girl's bed, my bedroom shrunk in half as my mother regaled me with stories of how she found solace buried beneath heavy quilts on this very bed.

It forces me to interact with people whom I loathe. People who pretend they are making a difference in the world. But seriously, what difference is made by stocking shelves, by pushing a broom, by scrubbing toilets? How is the world made a better place by pasting on a smile as an overweight, bitchy customer places their mouth an inch of your nose forcing you to smell the bacteria that hasn't been coated with the pleasing aroma of peppermint toothpaste in a week?

I detest the managers who sit on their asses sipping day-old coffee warmed in the microwave with their clipboards never out of arm's reach. If Alexander Fleming had a microwave in his lab, there is no doubt in my mind that he would have discovered penicillin years, if not decades, earlier. Managers are those people who convince themselves that they are better than us common laborers. But truth be told, they are more delusional. They must work extra hard to convince themselves that they are making a difference in the world. Or as my daddy liked to say (that was before he left our house in the middle of the night never to return), "They have to sit that high up to get away from the smell of their shit to convince themselves that their shit doesn't smell." I always thought that was a pretty futile effort, as I have yet to smell a pile of shit that didn't stink.

If it wasn't such a mind-numbing, meaningless burden, we wouldn't call it work! God, how I despise teachers and career counselors who once a year made the rounds of visiting each homeroom to discuss our futures and ask stupid questions like, "What do you want to be when you grow up or when you graduate?" What did they mean, "want to be?" I thought simply by breathing, I am. As if that wasn't bad enough, they would toss grenades of quotes at us. "Find a job you enjoy doing, and you will never have to work a day in your life." What was Mark Twain thinking when he uttered such blasphemy? Even better still, "Your work is going to fill a large part of your life, and the only way to be truly satisfied is to do what you believe is great work. And the only way to do great work is to love what you do." Easy enough for Steve Job to pontificate. Did these teachers really believe this stuff? Could they honestly look us in the eye and say they loved their work, when for the hundredth time they shouted, "Will you please shut up and listen? This is really important—it's your future!"

I hate that I have become a prostitute. I sell my services, as a laborer, as a peasant, in return for a few bucks. I am no different than a dog who performs tricks for the reward of a treat. A treat that must be earned based on the quality of my performance. If I question the tasks put before me, I am punished with extra duties or worse still, threatened with termination.

My God, I hate work, and I hate myself even more as I continue to play the game. I am nothing more than a cog in the machine of work.

* * *

"Hey, princess, break time is over." His monotone voice slapped her across the face. It's a voice she would prefer never to vibrate against her eardrum.

Without lifting her head to acknowledge his presence, her eyebrows rose just enough to view his mouth as he continued to disrupt her quiet time.

"Get back to work, or do you think because you're so special the floors will magically sweep themselves? Even Cinderella had to work."

"F… You." The words never passed her lips. Instead she spoke them again and again in her thoughts. The words that did fill the breakroom were her feeble efforts to garner more time. "I haven't finished my…"

"Too bad. Get back out there and make sure you smile."

Rolling her head back she looked directly into his eyes as she inquired, "Like this?" The slight upward curve of her lips was more of a flirtatious smile than a smile used to greet customers. It came naturally to her whenever she needed an older male to cut her some slack.

"Yeah, that will work." Following a momentary pause, he added, "And just in case you forgot, you close tonight." The manager's smile was equally flirtatious with just a hint of sarcasm as he tilted his head forward and narrowed his gaze.

"Aw, sh…" For a second time, she choked back her words, so they never escaped her mouth. Instead, she commented to the back of the manager's head who was passing the threshold of the doorway, "I completely forgot. I didn't pack a supper."

Without stopping, he delivered his response over his shoulder, "I guess today you are Cinderella."

Closing! That means mopping, cleaning the toilet, turning off the lights, and locking the doors.

Closing! If only it was just *cleaning* the toilet. Anyone who closed knew full well that the real task included a whole lot more than just cleaning. Cleaning is the surface stuff one does with a dust rag in hand as they dance about the house pushing the dust from tops of furniture. Cleaning consists of following behind a vacuum cleaner while listening to music through their earbuds. Cleaning the toilet during the day shift fits the definition of cleaning. It consisted of wiping the rim of the toilet to remove the dribbles of pee that resulted from males who impatiently concluded they had finished emptying their bladders. That wasn't the task of cleaning the toilet at closing.

Cleaning the toilet at closing means hosing down the toilet. Unfortunately, the store doesn't own a pressure washer. The long-handled scrub brush never seems long enough, and the bristles aren't sturdy enough to survive the porcelain pushback.

The Rerun Thrift Store was located two blocks north of the railroad tracks. It wasn't the roughest part of town, but it also wasn't the prettiest. Many of the storefronts stood vacant as the Westside Mall offered greater foot traffic. The apartments that once housed the merchants who operated businesses below had not been updated in decades. The complexion of those who do call the area home had darkened along with the streetlights that once lit the sidewalk.

The location of the Rerun Thrift Store served the needs of its clientele well. Those who contributed to the assortment of items by donating their unwanted stuff could do so just far enough away from their homes so that the likelihood of seeing the item again was minimal, and yet close enough so it was not a huge inconvenience to dump the items. Those who shopped at the store on a consistent basis appreciated its location, as most did not have transportation. The few customers who did drive to the store and visit once or twice a year let the employees know they were only in search of a costume or a gag gift.

The Rerun Thrift Store served additional purposes beyond offering items at cheap prices. In the winter, the store became a warming house, and in the summer, as the heat and humidity made life on the streets difficult, the store, with its multiple window air conditioners, offered cool freshness. But even more important was access to the porcelain thorn.

From the very first day that Marge opened the doors of Rerun Thrift Store, she refused to turn anyone away in need of the facilities. There was no sign posted reading *Public Restroom*, yet everyone in a four-block radius knew the facilities were public domain. Therefore, each night starting two hours before closing time, homeless guys who lived along the railroad tracks made their way into the store solely for the purpose of using the bathroom.

The duration of homelessness could be determined by how the bathroom was used. Those more recent to life on the streets, in addition to using the toilet, also used the sink and paper towels in an effort to remove the layers of street life. Others, having survived years of street life, recognized the futility of such efforts and avoided the sink. They also never forgot to flush.

Fortunately, attested to by every person who worked the late shift and closed the store, Marge posted several reminders in the small closet of a bathroom, *Flush!* She even employed creativity and humor to aid in the reminder. One sign read, *Please flush! This is not show and tell*. Another placed directly in front of the toilet stated, *Roses are red, Poop is brown, Flush it now, or we'll hunt you down*. The entire wall behind the toilet carried the message, *This magical poop-stealing water chair only works if you hold the handle down for 3 seconds*. As a result of Marge's interior design efforts, it was a rare occasion to be confronted by the brown remains of human waste.

Tonight will be no different, she told herself as the push broom glided across the wooden floor. Keeping her head tilted downward to avoid eye contact so she did not have to smile at customers, she still recognized the arrival of Harry. Not by sight, but by smell. If working at Rerun Thrift Store taught her anything it is the art of using her olfactory nerve more intently. Less than a month after starting the labors of work she realized that she could identify the patrons who stepped through the door by the odor that preceded their actual physical presence. Harry was one of the easiest as his sweaty heavy musky odor was combined with cheap whiskey. Most of the guys that called the railroad yard home drank cheap wine, but not Harry. Harry prided himself on the fact that he never lowered his standards to consume cheap, sweet wine. It was whiskey or nothing. Among the staff at the store, Harry was referred to as "The Thinker." Not because of the wisdom he shared but because of the amount of time spent in the bathroom. The joke is that one can set a stopwatch to Harry, and he will exit the bathroom after 48 minutes, give or take 10 seconds. Tonight, it is no different—47 minutes and 42 seconds.

Her stomach groaned announcing the absence of food. It had been a long day, longer than she planned when she left the comforts of her bed. The complaints from her belly were not anything she hadn't heard before. She frequently went for several days without consuming anything of substance. Food is highly overrated were the words she spit back at her mother whenever she was hounded to eat something. She was not sure why food wasn't pleasing or why she didn't crave certain foods like most people.

She unwrapped a stick of gum and chomped down while turning the deadbolt on the front door. A deep sigh followed. Now the real work begins, she mumbled as she filled the mop bucket. The only valuable bit of advice she received during orientation was that when you close, you always mop first and tackle the bathroom last. She wasn't sure why that order was necessary until the night of her first closing.

She stepped into the six-by-six space immediately after locking the front door only to escape backwards with her eyes filled with tears and her nose burning. The hour it took to mop the floor aided in airing out the bathroom.

On her second night of closing, she emptied an entire can of air freshener, Lavender and Peach Bloom, in the bathroom before starting to mop, but that made the situation worse as the stench now had moisture to cling to and it lingered longer. Plus, the sweet aroma mixed with BO and human waste seemed to penetrate her nose more deeply. The only way to survive the bathroom was to mop the entire store floor first, take a fresh stick of peppermint gum, and hold one's breath as long as possible.

Chapter 2

A soft yellow stream of light caught her eye as she reached back for the doorknob to pull the front door shut behind her. She knew immediately that the light originated from the makeshift dressing room. It was the only spot in the store that was lit by a single light bulb.

The dressing room was on the north wall of the store. The entrance, which was nothing more than a blue-colored sheet stapled over a three-inch long wooden dowel rod, split the shoe display wall rack in half. To the left were men's shoes and to the right were women's shoes. Reaching for the string without stepping into the dressing room, something flashed before the cornea of her eye that activated her retina. The string slid through her fingers, leaving the bulb to burn dimly, as she stepped back to view the wall of shoes. They were new arrivals; she had never noticed them before.

Shoes were her Achilles' heel, which sounded weird every time she uttered the notion because, with the right pair of shoes, the Achilles' heel would be protected. Nonetheless, shoes were the only thing that truly motivated her, and she knew it. Shoes, specifically a new pair of Vans Customs SK8-Hi Pro, were the only reason she worked. It was the only reason she dragged her butt out of bed. It was the only reason she hosed down the bathroom. The pair that flashed before her eye, that shimmered with elegance, was not a pair of Vans, but stilettos.

The ironic thing was that as much as she loved shoes, she refused to wear used shoes. She had never tried on a pair of shoes at the Rerun Thrift Store. In fact, her refusal to slide her foot into a shoe that another had worn cost her a date with the most popular junior in high school.

Brent Jacobson, star running back of the State Champion Football team, star wrestler, and the fastest person on the track team, slid up alongside her as she pulled books from her locker and casually, amongst the small talk, asked her out on a date. A date to go bowling. Bowling! Putting on bowling shoes! Shoes that had been on the feet of God knew how many other people!

Without looking directly into his eyes, the bluest eyes imaginable, she informed him that she had to go visit her grandma in the hospital who was gravely ill and therefore was unable to accept the invitation. It wasn't a total lie. Grandma was in the hospital. However, she wasn't on her deathbed; she was recovering from a hernia operation. The result of pushing too hard while seated on the toilet, or so Grandma told everyone who came to visit. She knew that if Grandma ever found out that her visit to the hospital cost her a date with Brent Jacobson, Grandma would eternally be upset with her. Grandma was cool like that, and it made her hope that coolness was a trait that skipped every other generation. Her mom was anything but cool!

Standing beneath the soft yellow glow of light holding the stiletto with an ankle strap and four-and-a-half-inch heel silenced her phobia. The wine-colored pointed toe screamed sexy, boldness, confidence, and attitude with a capital "A." If there was such a thing as coolness radiating from shoes, this was it! In the quietness of the empty store, she thought she heard the shoes whispering, "*Put me on. Put me on.*"

It took little effort to unlace and kick her feet free from her scuffed Doc Martens. Before carefully gliding her foot down the steep angle of the heels, she checked the size to determine how gracefully she could take that first step. Frustration pressed her shoulders down as she read a two-digit number, 10. She wore a seven. They were going to be too big.

The yellow light lost its glow of softness, and the milky glimmer mocked her childish desire to promenade about the store with class, sophistication, and sex. Who did she think she was? Cinderella? Her life did not offer any hope of a fairy tale ending. Life was offering the same outcome as waltzing about the store. An outcome of falling flat on her face. Yet she convinced herself that the ankle strap would keep the shoe attached to her foot.

The tips of her toes touched the lining of the stiletto and they tingled. Without thought she pulled her foot back. This is silly, she told herself. Again, she lowered her foot, and again her toes started to tingle, but she was prepared, and her foot effortlessly slid downward. As her toes reached the tip of the shoes the entire bottom of her foot was tingling. She wrapped the ankle straps around her ankle and fastened the straps to her prickly ankle. Before the second foot was strapped in, the tingling progressed up her leg. She tried to ignore the feeling, but the feeling of pins and needles didn't dissipate.

She could not explain what transpired but the moment she stood up the heels transformed to fit her feet perfectly. The size ten stiletto became a size seven. It felt as though she was someone else walking, dancing, strutting about the Rerun Thrift Store in the wine-colored stilettos with an ankle strap.

With one hand on the frame of the threshold, to balance herself, as her other hand pulled back the sheet. She stepped into the dressing room and turned left to observe herself in the full-length mirror. But the figure who stared back at her was that of another.

Chapter 3

Marge did not have many rules and regulations that she demanded the employees follow. Policies were not a priority for her. That wasn't true for the managers she hired. To secure their positions or to make sure others understood their position of power and dominance, they demanded strict compliance with policies, regardless of whether the policy even existed.

No, according to Marge, there were only two rules that absolutely had to be adhered to. Rule number one—every person who stepped through the door would be treated as a human being no matter how they looked, smelled, or acted. Rule number two—no mirrors were permitted to be displayed in the store. Marge repeatedly said people don't come to this store to look at themselves; they don't want reminders of how they might look. Those who want to look at themselves in a mirror have spent hours in front of a mirror before ever arriving at the store. They can survive 30 minutes without looking at themselves. If someone inquired about purchasing a mirror, they would be ushered back to the storeroom where they could rummage through shelves stocked with all shapes and sizes of mirrors. There was one exception to that rule. A full-length mirror was positioned strategically against the side wall of the dressing room, so it was visible only when one stepped into the space.

The figure in the mirror belonged to someone other than Bella. The tingling, the prickling sensation became overwhelming, and Bella felt light-headed and nauseous. Her body weaved back and forth. She was losing touch with reality; she felt weak. She was about to fall or, worse yet, faint. She stepped against the wall to center herself and breathe. Panic flooded her body. Where was her long black hair that concealed most of her face? Where was that slender figure? The only thing she recognized as belonging to her were the wine-colored stilettos. At that moment, she wasn't even sure they belonged to her.

Using the wall, she slid down to the floor and tried to keep the dressing room from spinning. Her entire world was spinning. What was happening? Why couldn't she see herself in the mirror? Who or what was in the mirror staring back at her? Why was that figure wearing the wine-colored, ankle strap stilettos? She continued to take deep breaths to keep from vomiting, but small amounts of acidic liquid rose from her stomach and settled in her mouth. Without knowing, tears fell from the corner of her eyes. She had to be dreaming. This was a nightmare. She must have fallen asleep. She needed to pull herself out of the dream.

But she wasn't dreaming. She hadn't fallen asleep.

She reached out and touched the ankle strap of the stiletto on her right foot. Without knowing why, she loosened the strap and removed the shoe and then the left one. The instant the second stiletto fell free of her foot, the figure in the mirror disappeared, the room stopped spinning, and the tingling was gone. The yellow light seemed brighter and hers was the only image in the mirror.

If she didn't know better, she might have concluded that she just came down from an acid trip. But drugs were not part of her repertoire. She hadn't had anything to eat or drink, so no one could have slipped her something. This didn't make any sense, and that was what scared her. The only thing she knew for sure was that strange, totally indescribable feeling.

She picked up one of the heels and carefully examined every inch of the shoe. Nothing. The other shoe revealed the same, nothing. Everything was the same, including the size.

Determined to reenact what transpired, she placed her foot in the stiletto and proceeded to secure the ankle strap. As she did her internal voice screamed, "*Bella, Bella are you crazy? Bella, what are you doing? Stop!*" Ignoring her voice, her other foot slid effortlessly into the shoe. Before the strap was tight, her feet tingled, the light dimmed, the room moved first left and then right, and a figure, the same figure stood firmly, boldly, with confidence and sex in the mirror.

Motivated by curiosity from within, she extended her arm toward the mirror. Discovering she was inches short of making contact with the glass, she tilted her torso forward. Not sure what to expect, her fingers floated millimeters above the surface until she reached the stilettos in the mirror. The tip of her index finger traced the outline of the shoes, first the right and the left. Nothing! Nothing happened. She was disappointed. Something, anything would have been better than nothing. Nothing didn't helped her to understand.

Her palm lay flat against the mirror as she rose to her knees and took in the whole form of the figure stuck in the glass. Without registering her actions, she whispered, "Who are you? Why are you here?" Disappointment increased to a level of frustration, for the figure didn't speak.

Standing, she stared first at the shoes upon her feet and then into the eyes of the figure as she directed her next question to herself, "Why is this happening to me? Me, of all people, me, Bella?"

Taking a step back she studied the figure in its entirety. Then stepping closer, the tip of her nose experienced the coldness of the glass, as she examined every feature of the figure intently. What first appeared to be boldness, confidence, and sex began to fade. That wasn't quite right. The images did not fade. They crumbled, dissolved, deteriorated as though they were nothing more than a surface layer concealing the identity beneath. As the metamorphosis continued, the figure—the woman whom Bella initially viewed as powerful and forceful, beaming with life—appeared as a slave to life.

Startled, Bella pushed herself away from the mirror as the woman no longer stood lifeless. She moved. Her movement was not simply of limbs. It was as though Bella was witnessing this woman moving through time. Her existence was on display for Bella to behold.

It started with the woman seated in an exclusive shoe store sliding her foot into a pair of wine-colored, ankle strap stilettos. Bella observed an innocence, a childlike expression covering the woman's entire body as she stood and admired the shoes on her feet for the very first time. It was so powerful that several customers in the store turned and inhaled her every step. It wasn't clear if she recognized or understood the power she possessed at that moment until she spoke. The voice that had informed the salesman that she "would like, like ah, you know, pair of them high like heels" delivered in a squeaky, fast-paced rhythm, now informed the same salesman with a husky, sultry, slow-paced delivery, "This pair will do simply fine. Be a love and toss my old shoes in the trash bin." She knew. She knew as she left the store and strolled down the sidewalk. She knew how to work the innocence, the childlike expression in her favor. Innocence became boldness, confidence, and sex.

As time pushed the woman further away from the moment when she first purchased the stilettos, the layers increased. Any resemblance to childlike expressions was gone. The twenty-something, blond-haired, full-figured woman became, with warp-like speed, thirty-something. Her two-room apartment became a penthouse with two cars parked in the underground garage. There was always a drink in hand or within reach. There was a heaviness and a shadow of darkness that appeared which had not been visible previously. The boldness, the confidence, and sex covered its presence, but there were moments, moments when the woman was alone, that something from within pressed to the surface.

Favors was the word Bella assigned to the scenes that followed. Favors that rolled forth from men of every shape and size. Favors never requested, but clearly expected. Favors from women of every shape and size. Favors seemed to be the link between the shoes and the lifestyle that flashed across the mirror.

The shift was subtle. The speed at which the scenes rolled through decades blurred the alteration of favors. Favors flipped from being *for* her to being *from* her. Bella noticed it immediately as the stilettos sat front and center in the closet. Seldom did the shoes leave the closet, seldom did the woman's feet gracefully slide into the four-and-a-half-inch heels. The shoes became meaningless in supplying favors. The woman became the source, the supplier of favors. Favors for every shape and size of men. Men looked at her not as a beautiful person, not even as a person, but as an object, a tool to satisfy a need. Women who would acknowledge her, who might be called "friends" were leeches, using her to increase their status. It was painful for Bella to witness because the woman in the mirror did not see it, she did not recognize the flip. And when she did…

The mirror turned black. No image, no figure was visible.

Belle sat and stared. Tears streamed down her cheeks. She laughed an uncomfortable laugh. She was crying for a figure, a figure of a woman stuck in the mirror. She cried because, *"My God, that could be me someday. ME! And if not me, then some other woman. A woman taught, beaten, violated, stripped, raped. Raped of dignity, of purpose, of life. A woman, any woman, all women who are forced to believe that they are nothing more than an object. An object to be used, to be worn."*

In the center of the mirror, a light flickered. And then again and again, and it grew in size each time the light flickered. The mirror was coming back to life. The figure of a woman slowly took shape. She was standing barefoot on the edge of a bridge and next to her was a pair of shoes.

The husky, sultry voice was gone. Replaced by a squeaky, fast-paced rhythm. Belle listened as the woman confessed that those shoes were nothing but objects she used to satisfy her insecurities. And now… now she was the shoe; she was an object. She had become the wine-colored, ankle strap stilettos…

The mirror again went dark
    Nothing
        Nothing
            Nothing
                Nothing
                    Nothing
                        Nothing
                            Nothing
                                Nothing

Bella touched the stilettos on her feet and contemplated removing them, but she stopped herself. She needed to be patient. She needed to know what happened. What happened to the woman, to the shoes? How did they get from the bridge to the Rerun Thrift Store? What happened to the woman?

Chapter 4

Her feet began to tingle. Just as they did earlier. The feeling of pins and needles progressed upward. She felt nauseous and light-headed. She thought about standing, about sticking her head outside the dressing room. The thought of moving was squelched as her head started to pound beneath an unrelenting pressure. Her chest ached. She labored to fill her lungs with air. She was too young for a heart attack, too young for a stroke, too young to die, at least that's what she told herself in the midst of what felt like a hammer striking her head.

Bella opened her mouth, prepared to scream *STOP!* when the mirror sprang to life.

On the edge of the mirror, the stilettos appeared. It was difficult to discern where the shoes were because all Bella could see were the shoes. Out of the darkness that consumed most of the mirror, except for the small spot where the shoes were, a hand, a wrinkled, worn hand, shaking lifted the wine-colored, ankle strap stilettos from the iron railing of the bridge.

The darkness pulled back across the face of the mirror, and Bella watched as the shoes came to rest on the bosom of a faceless figure. She concluded, as the shoes were carried forth, the bearer was not the woman who stood next to the shoes on the bridge, not the woman who once wore the shoes. She heard what sounded like whimpering that became wailing. As the scenery continued to change, she recognized different images of a city, her city. The shoes were in her hometown. And then she gasped as she read the signage *Rerun Thrift Store*.

She saw the front door, the inside of the store, the racks and racks of stuff. The shoes stopped moving when they reached the center of the store. For what seemed like forever, but was less than a minute, there was nothing. Slowly, clearly with reluctance, the shoes left the warmth of the bosom of the carrier and were placed in the waiting hands of Marge. Words followed that were difficult to hear as they were mingled with starts and stops controlled by crying. "These shoes once belonged to my daughter. They were her prized possession. Please take them and give them to another."

Bella allowed herself to acknowledge the emptiness within only when she stood outside the store. She was sad at the thought that she didn't work for another three days. She knew she couldn't tell anyone about what just happened, and that made her feel alone. Yet strangely mingled with the sadness and loneliness, there was a degree of excitement as she could not wait to once again visit the mirror.

* * *

Twenty minutes before she needed to report for work, Bella pushed through the front door and raced to the shelf of the women's shoes. Her ears never heard Marge's inquiry, "How was your weekend?"

Yet she spoke as she passed her boss. "The shoes..."

Curious how the response fit the question, Marge followed her youthful employee to the north wall. "Shoes?" Marge looked confused. "What about the shoes?"

"No. No, where are they? What happened to the shoes?" It was a silly question; any rational person would know the shoes were sold. However, Bella was not rational at that moment.

"What shoes are you talking about?"

"You know, the stilettos. The wine-colored, ankle strap stilettos. The four-and-a-half-inch heels that were on the top shelf. Where are they? Were they moved?"

"Sold." Marge turned and started to walk away.

"Sold? What do you mean sold? I mean, I mean, I know sold, but what? I mean, who?" She stepped back and hit the rack of oversized women's blouses. "Who bought them? Do you know? Do you remember?"

Marge didn't respond.

Drained of excitement and feeling nothing but sadness and loneliness she mumbled, "My God, I hate work."

Chapter 5

Over the course of the next month, returning to the Rerun Thrift Store became more and more challenging as the sole purpose for work. The motivation to mop, sweep, and scrape the poop from the toilet was gone. Bella no longer desired to own a pair of Vans Custom SK8-Hi Pro shoes. She struggled to place her feet in her own shoes.

She contemplated quitting but decided against the idea because besides, being a disappointment to her mom (nothing new), she realized she could not leave Marge. Marge had been good to her. She always made time to ask how she was doing, and it was more than small talk. She actually was interested in hearing her response. But even more, Bella knew that Marge would pester her for a reason why she was quitting, and if it were not the truth, Marge would know. She concluded one night as she drifted off to sleep, that she could live with disappointing her mom, but she wasn't sure she could live with disappointing Marge.

Luckily, a distraction from the events in the dressing room and the stilettos arrived in the form of Brent Jacobson. Much to her surprise and delight, Brent once again acknowledged her presence and, quite unexpectedly, would appear at her side in the hallway, at the water fountain, or beside her locker. She reveled in the attention and remained cautiously optimistic that an invite for a date was close at hand. Yet, fear gripped her throat, making it difficult to breathe: What if the invite was again a bowling outing?

It wasn't. He asked her to the movies.

The high school romance felt like a fairy tale. She questioned if she was playing the role of Cinderella and Brent was her prince charming. Charming he was. He would carefully slide his hand into her hand as they walked through the halls of school. He picked her up each morning and drove her to school. Since he had practice after school, he offered her his car, and said he would have a teammate drop him off at her house to retrieve his vehicle. She declined the offer because she didn't have a license. He didn't care. It's just a piece of paper, he would tell her. Eventually, she had to admit that she also didn't know how to drive. So on weekends, he started teaching her.

She had everything she ever hoped for in a relationship. Everything she dreamed. She was living in a state of being awake.

The theme of the Junior/Senior Prom was *Paradise* after the Coldplay song by the same title. Brent and Bella joked about dressing up in an elephant costume and arriving, each riding a unicycle, to copy the music video, but were happy they decided against it when half the people attending prom dressed as elephants and rode unicycles. Instead, the couple made their entrance in formal attire, Bella with a new pair of shoes her mother purchased just for the occasion.

The shopping excursion for the shoes had been stressful. Bella's mom was insistent that the proper shoe to accomplish the formal gown was a pair of high heels.

"The heels will not only add height and accentuate your gorgeous figure, they will also lift the bottom of the gown so it sweeps across the floor with each stride rather than mopping the floor."

"Mom, I don't need any additional height," Bella pleaded. "Plus, this is a dance, and I can't dance in heels. You want me to make a spectacle of myself as I fall and embarrass Brent?"

"Well, if it's a question of dancing, you can practice. If you are worried about falling, you will fall if your gown is dragging on the floor. I remember my junior prom…"

"Mom, this isn't your prom. Just be thankful Brent and I aren't going dressed in an elephant costume."

The evening was enchanting. They danced nearly every dance and Bella never fell once as her almond-colored mid-wedge shoes, complete with a bow, carried her effortlessly. They laughed. They sipped the punch from the bowl spiked with vodka. They kissed at the end of each dance, and they kissed during the slow dances. The relationship transcended the boundaries of a high school fling. The word *love* was at the back of their throats waiting, anticipating the perfect moment that it might escape.

When the lights flooded the dance floor, the PA system squeaked to life, and the principal announced that it was one minute past twelve and that the dance was over, Brent held Bella close and whispered, "Let's skip the after-prom party."

"But, but, can we do that?" It was less an objective than an inquiry for permission.

"Sure, we just don't show up."

"I don't know…" For Bella, not showing up was different from being given permission. Was it okay to not attend even though they had signed up?

"I thought we could drive out to the lake and watch the sunrise."

Bella's body began to tingle. It was the same feeling she felt the moment she slipped on the wine-colored stilettos. The feeling spread. She wasn't sure what she thought, only that her body was a mass of confusion. Was the stirring within excitement or fear, apprehension or anticipation, anxiety or exhilaration?

In the end, looking deep into Brent's eyes, those blue eyes, trusting him, she leaned against his head and whispered, "Yes, yes, I want this evening to continue, just you and me."

* * *

Parked beside the lake that just lost the last chunks of ice only a week earlier, they elected to remain in the car. The blanket Brent pulled from the backseat covered their bodies rather than the sand on the beach. Bella leaned back against Brent as he reclined back against the door. The sunroof in Brent's car enabled the couple to gaze at the stars and imagine that they were outside.

With his arms wrapped around her body, she felt safe. What initially felt awkward about being alone in the middle of the night, five miles from town, now felt right. So right that as her eyes grew heavy with sleep, she didn't fight it but pressed deeper into Brent's chest and fell asleep.

Time has no meaning when one sleeps, so she had no idea how long she had been asleep when she woke quite suddenly. She felt her body jerk and then jump before she realized she was waking up before she opened her eyes. The interior of the car was dark, but she didn't need to see to know she was uncomfortable.

Brent's right hand had pushed down the front of her dress slipped inside her bra and cupped her left breast, while somehow his left hand breached the top of her panties. She instinctively lifted his hand out of her bra and with greater difficulty pulled his other hand out of her panties, while saying, "No."

"I'm sorry, I just thought, I mean, … Bella, I love you." As he spoke to the back of her head, he again cupped her breast. "I want to feel your body. I want to make love to you too."

"Stop it!" The pitch of her voice climbed higher. Her heart was racing, not with excitement but with fear and panic. She lifted herself off him and curled up against the passenger's door.

For a moment, there was silence. Even the wind, which had been blowing off the lake, seemed to take offense at what had just happened, and it too pulled back.

Brent again spoke and started with an apology, but Bella stopped him. "Please, let me share with you my thoughts." Brent nodded and Bella continued. "I have never felt anything like I feel for you. I think it's love, but honestly, I don't know for sure because no one has ever told me this is what love is supposed to feel like. But Brent, even if it is love that doesn't mean I am ready to make love with you." She raised her hand to stop his objection. "And if I were going to give myself to you, I want to be a part of the decision."

Brent turned and rested his head on the steering wheel. Bella wasn't sure if he was hurt or angry. Even though she was awake this time, she still could not determine the amount of time that elapsed before Brent dropped back in the seat and looked at her.

"I don't know what to say, Bella. No one has ever said no to me or told me to stop."

"You've had sex before?"

"Yeah, of course."

"And your whole reason for coming out here was to have sex?"

He didn't answer at first. His response was a simple nod of his head. And then he spoke in an attempt to explain, to justify his answer. "I thought you wanted to as well."

Fighting back tears and trying not to let him know she was crying deep inside, she asked him to take her home.

"Ah, Bella, we don't have to…"

"I would like to go home." Afraid he might try to convince her to stay with him in the car, she thought about the walk back to town. Five miles was a long way and at this hour, no one was going to come along and offer her a ride.

His hand reached out and touched her arm, an arm she had wrapped about her legs. The very touch that only hours before she longed to feel felt wrong and unwanted. She didn't pull back from his touch, but she also did not affirm it. She sat as still as a rabbit in the presence of a fox. He lifted his hand and placed it on the key in the ignition and started the car.

The five-mile drive back into town and to her house seemed to take forever. Neither spoke until they arrived.

"I really am sorry, Bella. You are like no one I have ever met. I truly mean that. I wasn't lying when I said, 'I think I love you.' Can I call you tomorrow?"

Bella didn't answer. She pushed the door open and escaped from inside Brent's car. She ran across the yard barefoot, holding up the bottom of her formal so it neither mopped nor swept the ground.

She left her almond-colored wedge shoes under the front seat of the car.

Chapter 6

Summer could not arrive quickly enough. Bella needed a break from school, from the teachers, from the other students, and especially from encountering Brent throughout the day, every day. Their relationship never officially ended, but only in part because Bella refused to take any of Brent's phone calls. She refused to respond to his texts. Whenever he attempted to speak with her, her responses were nothing more than one-word responses, *Yeah*, *No*, and *Maybe*. With an occasional shrug of her shoulders followed by, "So."

Summer also allowed Bella's internal clock to reset, which for Bella didn't follow solar time. Her sleeping cycle did not align with the circadian clock. If she had to be to work by 9 am she would drag her butt out of bed by 8:40 am. If she didn't work, noon was considered early. She was thankful for a large bladder.

For the first time, Bella was thankful for her job. It served as a distraction. Closing no longer bothered her. She volunteered to close whenever scheduled to work. It was a way to avoid her mom who tirelessly pestered her to start making some decisions concerning her future.

"You are a senior now. What will you do after graduation?" The words became her mom's mantra. Over and over, she spoke the words as though if she said them enough, an answer would magically appear.

The response from Bella was always the same. "I don't know." She really didn't know. She had been avoiding the thought. It was scary to think about leaving home, about attending college, about having to meet new people, and possibly making new friends. Even worse than the thought of college was contemplating life after college. What did she want to do, or as some people might ask, what did she want to be? Her honest response, but never uttered because it sounded too sarcastic and she feared few would understand, was, "I already *am*, I don't need to *be*." But it scared her to consider that she would have to grow up.

She also looked forward to going to work because she allowed herself to become more open with Marge. Marge had a personality like a golden retriever. Everyone felt comfortable talking with her. She made time for everyone and not because she owned the store or felt sorry for some of the patrons. She didn't pity anyone. No, Marge truly cared for all human beings, and one felt it the moment she greeted them.

Bella had always felt relaxed in Marge's presence, but she still held herself back. The summer, however, offered an opportunity to talk about more than work duties. One day in particular challenged Bella to stop and consider the choices she made every day.

"Kinda hot for those Doc Martens, isn't it?"

Bella wasn't sure the question was directed at her, as she had been minding her own business while finding the mismatched pairs of shoes. When she turned around, she noticed Marge was three aisles away picking up clothes from the floor and putting them back on hangers. Certain that the question wasn't for her, she went back to searching for a Converse tennis shoe, size five.

"Your feet so sweaty that it's affecting your hearing?"

As Bella turned, she saw that Marge was looking straight at her. "Sorry, I didn't know if you were talking to me or someone else."

"You see anyone else in Doc Martens? It's too hot for those boots."

Bella smiled; she liked the way Marge would banter without being offensive. Her honesty was always expressed for the purpose of goodwill. It also permitted her to shovel it back. "Well, if the dress code wasn't so restrictive, I wouldn't have to wear them."

"Restrictive?" Marge laughed.

Before she could say another word, Bella continued, "I can't go barefoot, so I'm stuck wearing Doc Martens."

"I'll bet you a full day's wages that you never thought about what shoes you would wear today. You just reached for the Doc Martens, pulled them on, and laced them up. Am I right?"

"First of all, I don't bet. But, yeah, I suppose, sort of… you're right."

"Why do you think that is?"

With a shrug of her shoulders and a slight tilt of her head, Bella said, "I don't know. They were next to my bed?"

"Why don't you wear something more comfortable, something cooler? Maybe a pair of flip-flops?"

"Flip flops? You would actually allow flip-flops?"

"Have I ever said flip-flops are unacceptable?"

"No, but… flip-flops? I can't see myself wearing flip-flops?"

Moving to the next aisle to search for clothes beneath the rack, Marge continued to press Bella. "What's wrong with flip-flops?"

"What do you mean, what's wrong? Just the word, flip flops, says it all."

"And what do Doc Martens say?"

"You know what I mean."

"This may come as a surprise, but I don't. Let me ask, have you ever worn flip-flops?"

Without giving it any thought, she answered, "No." That was not true. She had worn flip-flops as a young child. The ones from the five-and-dime store that lasted for a day before the stem pulled through the base of the shoe. To her credit, she didn't lie. She honestly didn't remember the four pairs of flip-flops her mom purchased that summer when she was four.

"Perhaps before you are critical and judgmental you need to wear a pair."

"Like that's going to happen."

Having delivered a final comment, "Well, I'm just saying," Marge exited the aisle and went to the other side of the store to continue her efforts of tidying up the store.

Returning to face the north wall in search of mixed-matched pairs of shoes, Bella mumbled to herself, "Flip flops? Why would I ever wear flip-flops?"

* * *

Alone in the store, having finished mopping the floor and hosing down the bathroom, Bella once again stood before the north wall and stared at a pair of flip-flops. The pair was to the left of the dressing room sheet, meaning that they were identified as male footwear. That seemed rather silly, since, if there was such a thing as gender-neutral shoes, flip-flops would fit the definition. Yet there they were. She assumed they were placed on that side of the sheet because they resembled mini skis. They had to be at least a size 13, maybe larger. Earlier in the evening, during her supper break, she asked Marge if she could borrow her iPad. While nibbling on a cheese sandwich, Bella researched the origins of flip-flops. Much to her surprise, there was site after site that described the history of flip flops, also called thongs. Bella had assumed that the simple design made its initial appearance in the Sixties with the hippies or beach bums. She discovered that the simple footwear design goes back to early civilizations, while the more current flip flop arrived in the United States following WWII, as soldiers returning from Japan brought the shoes back with them. For some reason, that single piece of information permitted Bella to try a pair of flip-flops.

Staring at the shoes her thoughts flipped back to the wine-colored stilettos. She wasn't sure what might happen if she were to put the shoes on the floor and place her foot on the rubber-like substance. She decided that she would start outside the dressing room but have the light on in the dressing room in case she wanted to look in the mirror. One thing was absolutely clear: Her bare foot would never, absolutely never, touch the surface of the flip-flop. Her socks would remain on.

The presence of the socks made it more difficult to get the thong (the stem) comfortably placed between her big toe and second toe. The moment the thong butted up against the crease between her toes, the room started to turn. Unlike with the stilettos, there was no tingling, no pins and needles. Instead, there was music in her ears, the sound of which increased with each step she took. The flapping noise of the rubber-like substance striking first the wooden floor and then her heel was barely audible, as all sounds were muffled and drowned out by the music that rang in her ears.

She didn't recognize the music, but it sounded old. She wasn't sure why; it just did. It sounded like something Grandma would enjoy. Yes, that's it. Bella remembered when she was little and she stayed at Grandma's house. At least once, sometimes more, they had to watch a movie with some guy named Elvis. The movie took place in Hawaii, and Grandma reminded her that, at the time of the movie, Hawaii was not yet a state. That was the sound, beach-type music.

After a trip that took her down one aisle and back up another, Bella stood before the dressing room sheet and deliberated the risk factors associated with stepping inside. The risk was not physical but emotional. If she experienced anything like she did with the wine-colored. ankle strap stilettos, she would be left mentally exhausted. For days, she had replayed what unfolded in the mirror, and there were unanswered questions. But…

Pushing the sheet to the right, she stepped in and turned to face the mirror. She squinted, narrowing the range of her vision, in an attempt to control the amount of the image she observed. But there was no image. She waited and waited some more. Her shoulders started to ache from standing, staring, and being tense that at any minute the owner of the flip-flops would flash before her eyes. But there was no image.

When she rolled her shoulders to ease the tension, it occurred to her that there was no music playing in her ears. Turning and staring at the back side of the sheet, she realized that the music stopped the moment she entered the dressing room. With the anticipation of seeing a figure in the mirror, the music was not immediately missed. Now, its absence was haunting, disconcerting.

Her head dropped to her chest in disappointment. She felt foolish, worse yet, idiotic that she allowed herself to think that by simply sliding her foot into a used pair of shoes, flip flops no less, she would meet the previous owner.

She shook her head several times, reached for the sheet with one hand, and grabbed the string dangling from the yellow light bulb as she stepped to exit the dressing room. Before she could free herself from the now dark dressing room, a faint light, an image, flickered in the upper right-hand corner of the mirror. It reminded her of the light from a laser pointer. She gently pulled herself back into the tiny space. The glowing dot slowly moved toward the center of the mirror. As it did, the dot grew in intensity.

Bella kept her eyes fixed on the glowing dot, squinting occasionally, expecting a fireworks explosion. It felt as though she were back in her Advanced Placement psychology course where the instructor had the class stare at a brightly colored picture until another image, a concealed image, rose out of the colored blocks and circles. The words of encouragement from the instructor rattled about in her head, "Relax, relax, and the image will appear."

As the light neared the center of the mirror, it now covered more than three-quarters of the surface. Like the action, while wearing the wine-colored stilettos, she leaned against the wall across from the mirror and took a seat on the floor. The added space revealed the image that had been concealed.

The body and the face belonged to an old man, a worn man, a tired and lonely man who sat on a metal chair hunched forward. Unlike the woman who wore the stilettos and stared out from the mirror and whose eyes Bella could search, the old man did not look outward, his eyes not immediately visible. His attention was directed toward four picture frames that were placed across the table. Between him and the photos were a glass ashtray heaped with cigarette butts, a pack of Marlboros, and a shiny silver lighter engraved with the name *George*.

Through the blue-gray fog of cigarette smoke, the profile of the old man revealed that attached to his bare feet were flip-flops. His toes were gnarly and the toenails jagged and uneven as though he did not own a nail clipper but simply tore the nail when it was too long. The faces in the photos behind a thick film of soot were that of women. Family members, Bella concluded, as they all possessed similar features. The photo on the left appeared to be the oldest as it was black and white. The young woman was seated on the steps of a church with the hem of her wedding dress covering several steps. This was probably a picture of the old man's bride, Bella told herself.

The other three pictures looked to be that of a graduation, perhaps, high school or college; it wasn't discernable. There were no names attached to the photos, but why would there be if these were the old man's daughters? Surely, he knew their names. He knew each of them by sight, by actions, by… Bella pulled attention away from the photos. She tried to look beyond the table, past the old man to see if there was any evidence that any of these people resided in the house. There was none.

Her focus was pulled back to the table as the old man, a man she would call George, reached for the pack of cigarettes. He tapped the box against the palm of his left hand, removed the celophane wrapping, flipped the lid of the box open, and pulled a cigarette out. He tossed the Marlboro box back on the table and picked up the silver lighter. He used the palm of his left hand to tap the lighter. With a slight upward action of his thumb, the cover flipped open, and his thumb rolled across the inside of the lighter. A flame leaped upward that he directed to the end of the cigarette. George inhaled deeply, the end of the cigarette glowed with heat, he dropped back against the chair, and smoke drifted out of his nose as his head tilted back. Effortlessly, without looking, he flicked his wrist back bring the cover of the lighter fell forward. It snapped shut, and the old man tossed it toward the ashtray.

Bella had never paid much attention to the act of lighting a cigarette. It surprised her how much was involved in the act and how much comfort was supplied by the ritual of smoking. As George reclined, he crossed his feet, and the right flip-flop hung free from his foot. Mindlessly, working the toes of his right foot, the flip-flop sprang to life moving to and fro from his foot. Rather than pulling his torso away from the back of the chair to reach the ashtray in the center of the table, he used his pants leg to hold the ash of the cigarette. The palm of the left hand pressed the ash into the fabric of the pants.

As the end of the cigarette burned toward the filter, the action of the flip-flop slowed until he uncrossed his feet, leaned forward, and smashed the butt into the ashtray. The action caused several butts to be pushed from the ashtray and onto the tabletop.

From the dead, completely smoked cigarette, George's hand reached for the Marlboro box, and the whole scene repeated itself. Bella felt the hopelessness of George's existence. The soles of her feet were numb. If she had not been seated, she was sure she would have toppled over. To an existence as futile as George's, feet served little purpose. Overwhelmed by the vainness of life that hemorrhaged from his body, she wanted to pull free of the flip-flops. She had seen enough, but she couldn't look away because the rest of her body wanted to know what led to this moment. The flip-flops clung to her feet because George's body wanted, needed another human being to know the story.

The story did not appear within the confines of the mirror but materialized within Bella's body. In her mind's eye, she saw the image of a young man, a twenty-something, a well-groomed gentleman, unwrapping a gift. The scene transpired while the old man, trapped in the mirror, puffed away at his Marlboros like a coal-fired steam locomotive.

Bella drifted from the old man in the mirror and centered on the young man carefully opening the package so as not to tear the wrapping paper. She became aware that hopelessness gave way to excitement. Her stomach was no longer heavy with grief but fluttered with butterflies. As the youthful man smiled holding the unwrapped gift in his hands, she smiled.

The gift was a first-anniversary wedding gift from his wife. Held in his hands was a pair of flip-flops.

Due to the financial restraints of being recent college graduates, and unemployed at the time of the wedding, the couple could not afford a honeymoon. Both having secured employment and harboring a few dollars from every paycheck, the couple was able to afford a four-day, three-night stay in a cabin on a lake. The gift of flip-flops was meant to be a practical gift George could make use of during and after their honeymoon. George's gift for his lovely wife, a two-piece bikini, served two purposes. It was practical for swimwear and tantalizing enough to remind the couple this was their honeymoon. The bikini served its purpose well. Two months after the three-night trip to the lake, the couple learned that they were expecting their first child.

While the bikini faded with time and lost its alluring powers, the flip-flops did not lose their appeal. They remained a mainstay packed for every yearly vacation no matter where the family traveled. A family that expanded from three to five over seven years. The footwear made countless appearances on the concrete streets as George marched protesting racial inequalities and the Vietnam War.

The flip-flops transformed George from an attorney confined to a stuffy office pushing papers to an activist. Someone who challenged the law rather than interpreting the law. Someone who joined the voice of the common man rather than giving voice to the corporate world. Someone who was arrested and thrown in jail rather than the one who kept wealthy clients out of jail.

Bella has never felt such passion, such enthusiasm, such a sense of civic duty. The idea of civil disobedience in government class was nothing more than a term on a midterm final. But wearing George's flip flops, the very shoes that Marched on Washington, that were present as Martin Luther King Jr. delivered *I Have a Dream*, the footwear sprinkled with the spray of blood as a cop's baton found George's forehead amid a crowd singing, "We Shall Overcome," tiny droplets of salty water escaped from the corners of Bella's eyes.

For a moment she looked at the figure in the mirror finishing his fifth cigarette and whispered, "What happened to you? Where is that passion, that enthusiasm, that purpose for living? The flip-flops are still on your feet. How can you just sit there and slowly kill yourself?"

She paused for several seconds and then added one final thought, "Or, are you already dead, and your body just doesn't know it? Perhaps, it's the flip-flops that refuse to allow you to die."

Of course, the old man never responded to her questions. He never so much as turned to acknowledge her presence. He stared at the four picture frames, pulled another cigarette from the box, and went about the task he could complete without thought.

The inside of a 1975 Ford LTD Country Squire Station Wagon, green in color and trimmed with wood side panels, was an endless cocoon of noise. Over the song "Get Down Tonight" by KC and Sunshine Band that woofed from the speakers, the two youngest daughters, in the seat directly behind Mom and Dad, screamed at each other about whose turn it was to play with the Barbies, and the oldest daughter, now a teenager, shouted at her mother how lame the trip was. In addition, Mom, the co-pilot for the harrowing trip, was offering directions to George when he needed to turn off the interstate.

"George, in ten more miles you need to exit. George, are you listening to me? Only nine more miles. If you miss the exit ramp, there is not another exit for twenty-two miles. George…"

George, wearing his flip-flops with black socks and blue-and-white plaid Bermuda shorts just smiled. This wasn't noise. This was the sound of family togetherness. Unfortunately, it would be the last time a family vacation contained these voices. Fortunately George couldn't predict the future, and he basked in the sound of family.

Two months after the family returned home from their trip to the Rocky Mountains and Yellowstone National Park, George's wife became ill. She was diagnosed with breast cancer. The autopsy a month later revealed that what initially was thought to be breast cancer was everywhere cancer. It had consumed her entire body.

George tried for several years to wear the flip-flops and load the girls into the station wagon for a family vacation, but the definition of family had changed. The girls pushed back, and the sounds inside the vehicle were no longer the sounds of family but noise.

Even for George, the thought of sliding his feet into the flip-flops was just too much.

Bella, examining the old man's face again, contemplated the possibility that this was the source of hopelessness that rested heavily upon George's heart, and the weight she felt within her own body. But that didn't make sense. The flip-flops were on his feet. There must be more, something else pushed him into a state of not living.

In the tiny hands of a little girl, Bella watched as the flip-flops were transported from the dark recesses of the closet to George who, with a hoe in hand, was weeding a garden. The child spoke, "Grandpa, what are these?"

In total shock, as if seeing a ghost from the past, George asked, "Where did you find those?"

"In the house, in the back of a closet?"

"What were you doing in the closet?"

"I was playing."

"Playing?"

"Hide and seek with Mommy."

George knelt next to his granddaughter, scooped her up along with the flip-flops, and proceeded to tell her the story of how her grandma bought those shoes for him when they were young, just like her mommy.

"Why don't you wear them?"

The question stopped him. He swallowed and offered, "I don't know?"

"May I wear them?"

"Yes, yes, you may wear them." Beaming from ear to ear, George lowered his granddaughter to the ground, removed her shoes, and placed the flip-flops on her tiny feet. "Be careful! They are big."

The little girl slowly stepped with her right foot and then left and over and over, gaining her balance to the point she discovered it worked best to shuffle her feet across the grass.

George laughed as he watched his granddaughter. Bella felt a warming in her heart that George must have felt in that moment.

At about the same moment, his three daughters, home for the Fourth of July, all emerged from the house. When they saw the flip-flops on Sarah's tiny feet, each stopped moving forward. Sarah's mom spoke for George's daughters, "Oh, Dad, where did you find those? We thought you threw those away. Sarah, get your feet out of those stinky old things."

Bella's heart ached; she didn't need to see George's face to know the knife that just cut into his existence.

His daughters could not see what Sarah saw. They could not understand, or worse yet, refused to understand that the flip-flops were his life. The soul of his existence.

George never responded to his daughters' objection to the flip-flops. He merely pulled a pack of cigarettes from his shirt pocket, lit one, and then knelt to assist his granddaughter in removing the flip-flops.

Her face washed by her tears, Bella looked at the old man in the mirror and marveled that he too didn't weep daily. As he leaned forward to stub out the last remains of a cigarette, she noticed, for the first time, something sticking out of his shirt pocket. Before George reached for the pack of cigarettes, he pushed the chair back from the table, so his feet were visible. He stared at the flip-flops for several moments and then reached for the item tucked in the pocket of his shirt.

The item George pulled from his pocket was a 2x3 inch school picture of Sarah. He smiled, wiggled his toes, put the picture back in his shirt pocket, pulled the chair closer to the table, and reached for the pack of Marlboros.

Chapter 7

Bella was relieved to discover that the flip-flops were on the shelf right where she left them two days earlier. She had not slept well the two previous nights, in part for fear that, like the wine-colored stilettos that were sold, the flips flops would be gone. But her dreams both nights also had been possessed by the little girl Sarah. Sarah who was only part of the final chapter of the story revealed through the flip flops.

The daylight hours had not been any less stressful. She rehearsed over and over how she could persuade Marge to allow her to purchase the flip-flops. Marge had a store policy that employees were not to purchase items unless they were in desperate need or planned to pass the item on to a person in need. Bella realized her situation didn't fit either criteria, yet still she rehearsed. Even during the initial hours of her afternoon shift, she continued to brainstorm plausible scenarios of why she should be permitted to purchase the flip-flops. She concluded that the transition between greeting Marge and seeking Marge's approval was the key.

Bella was still thinking about the flip-flops when Marge strolled up behind her and asked, "Bella, you okay? You look as though you are distracted by something."

Bella's scrambled brain raced to respond and still be able to direct the conversation to the flip-flops. She answered, "No, I... I'm fine. Didn't sleep very well last night. I guess I'm a little tired."

Expressing her concern, Marge offered, "It's a pretty light afternoon, and we are well-staffed. You're welcome to go home and take a nap."

"Thank you for the offer, but I'll be okay." Bella forced a smile.

"Well, at least go outside for a few minutes and get some fresh air. Maybe that will wake you up, shake the cobwebs from your head." Marge was moving toward the front door as she spoke but then drew up short and quickly turned and faced Bella. She said, while looking down at her Doc Martens, "Though, that's probably not a good idea, the heat will only make you hot and more tired."

Bella could not keep from smiling. She now had the transition she needed. "You remember our conversation from the other day?"

Stepping closer to Bella, Marge said, "I'll need a bit more information to remember which conversation."

Bella spoke fast as excitement loosened her tongue. "About flip-flops and having cool feet."

"I recalled something about flip-flops. I don't remember everything."

"I told you how I had never worn flip-flops. Well, I was wondering if I could buy that pair of flip-flops that are on the wall."

Marge turned and scanned the wall to the right of the dressing room. "We have flip-flops? I don't remember getting in any flip-flops recently." She stepped toward the north wall and then walked three-quarters of the way down the aisle before she stopped and reported, "Sorry, Bella, but I don't know what flip-flops you are referring to."

"No, on the left side, in the men's section. Half the way up." Bella was pointing as she walked toward the shoes.

The two met in front of the flip-flops, and Marge pulled the pair from the rack on the wall. "Oh, these. They're men's aren't they? They look rather large for your small feet."

Bella pleaded her case, "Flip-flops are flip-flops. No one really notices if they are for males or females. And too big is better than too small."

Examining the shoes more closely, Marge said, "Flip-flops aren't the sort of footwear that sells very fast in secondhand stores. I think this pair arrived here two, maybe three years ago. I suppose we can make an exception this one time." Her final two words were accomplished by holding up one finger.

"Thank you, Marge. I really appreciate it."

"I am confident that the pair will be put to very good use." Marge smiled and then smirked as she handed the flip-flops to Bella and walked off.

Bella tilted her head and watched Marge walk away wondering what she meant by that.

Chapter 8

A week after Bella bought and took the flip-flops home and buried them beneath a pile of junk in her closet, Marge inquired about the shoes.

"How are those flip-flops working out?"

"Good. You were right. They are a little big, but I am getting used to them."

"So maybe when the summer is over, I'll see you wearing them in the store?"

"Yeah, I think so." Bella turned to leave hoping to end any further discussion about the flip-flops when Marge changed the topic from flip-flops to baby shoes.

"Yesterday we got in a pair of baby shoes. We don't get many pairs of baby shoes. Rather surprising since they seldom get worn out. Might have something to do with our clients. Do you remember your first pair of shoes?"

"Nah, I don't. Do you?"

" I do. My mother had my first pair of baby shoes bronzed and attached to a platform that included a picture frame. Of course, the picture is of me wearing the shoes."

"People really did that?"

"Yep, and just to be clear, I did it for my daughter as well."

"I'm so glad my mom never did that for me."

"Why?'

"I don't know. It just seems weird, you know, shoes bronzed.

"The pair we received yesterday are still in the backroom. Will you sanitize them, and if needed, add a bit of polish?"

"Sure, you want me to do that right now or later?"

"You close today, right?"

"Yep. Hosing down the bathroom."

Marge looked at Bella for a long second before responding. "Okay then. Just make sure the shoes are out on the rack for tomorrow morning."

Bella's other tasks, set out for her by Ronald, kept her occupied for the majority of her shift. As a result, she totally forgot about the shoes until she was scrubbing poop from the rim of the toilet. A strange connection, baby shoes and poop on the rim of the toilet… but then again, maybe not. Bella babysat for a few kids in the neighborhood over the years and changed enough diapers to understand the connection.

Having completed the closing duties, Bella went to the backroom in search of a pair of baby shoes. It took her several minutes to locate the shoes because, for some reason, Bella envisioned the baby shoes to be white in color, leather in texture, and with shoestrings. What she finally found was a bright purple pair of high tops, complete with vegan leather, cotton lining, faux fur to cover the ankle, and a natural rubber sole from the milk of the Hevea tree. The size stamped inside the shoe was as clear as if the shoe had never been placed upon a foot. It read *6-12 Months*.

As Bella sprayed the inside of each shoe with the disinfectant, she couldn't remember seeing an assortment of baby shoes being placed on the north wall. She was quite sure if a customer was in search of infant footwear, this pair would be snatched immediately. They were adorable.

Finding what she considered the perfect spot to display the shoes, Bella stepped back to make sure the shoes would catch the customer's eye. It was then that her thoughts took her to a place she hadn't expected, a place she hadn't prepared to visit. Was it possible that these tiny shoes could be transformed to fit her foot? It worked with shoes that were too large for her feet, so why not...

She told herself that was nonsense. What story would such shoes have to tell? A baby, six to twelve months of age, having a story to tell... how ridiculous. Besides, she wasn't sure she was done with the story of the flip-flops.

She shook her head twice and widened her eyes as though she was attempting to absorb reality. Yet she spoke to herself as though she had become two people. *"Listen to yourself. You are questioning the likelihood of a baby having a story to tell, rather than the logic of putting on a pair of infant shoes to see if they fit. You don't even question any longer how it is possible to meet the owner of the shoes. You just expect it. Are you mad?"*

Answering herself, she said, *"To be mad would be to pretend, to deny that something beyond comprehension has happened to me. To be mad would be to try and provide a rational explanation for irrational occurrences. To be mad would be to stop trying on shoes."*

Bella grabbed the infant shoes from the wall rack, pulled aside the sheet, yanked the string for the overhead light, slid down the wall opposite the mirror, removed her Doc Martens, and crammed her oversized foot into the opening of the purple high tops.

The moment the pair of purple high tops with faux fur and rubber soles made from the milk of a Hevea tree converted in size to accommodate Bella's feet, Bella's eyesight was restricted. The mirror across the tiny room was a blur. She could not discern any objects outside the dressing room. Her world consisted of a three-foot boundary.

She sat still for several minutes with her eyes closed hoping they would readjust and return to her 20/20 vision. It didn't work. The world she previously knew narrowed and closed in upon her. To add to the transformation, it was not only her sight that was altered, but all her senses changed. Her perception of reality was equal to what existed at the moment, the here and now, anything beyond, anything outside the immediacy of the moment did not exist. Anything unfamiliar was a threat to existence. And worse of all was the sense of abandonment. If another human being did not reside within the reality of three feet, there was no hope, no security, no food, no... anything.

Pressing against the wall, Bella unconsciously attempted to escape the confinement of such an existence. This was worse than watching George smoke cigarette after cigarette or seeing the stilettos alone on the bridge where once a person stood. She questioned if this was the definition of hell. It felt like it, from the bottom of her feet to the top of her head. The difference, of course, was that hell never ceases, whereas an infant would grow out of this narrow vision of life. For the moment, with the purple high tops upon her feet, this was life for Bella.

She pushed herself away from the wall and scooted forward, placing herself closer to the mirror. The images in the mirror slowly took shape, but only those within three feet of the tips of the purple high shoes that were slightly off-center. Items beyond the boundary were blurry and appeared to be covered with a haze. Bella's level of frustration increased due to the constraint placed upon her vision.

Periodically, one or both purple high tops would move, would shake, and Bella's attention was drawn to that point in hopes of seeing the infant whose feet were in the shoes. But all she saw were the shoes.

There were occasions when the sight of the shoes was hidden by an object that appeared out of nowhere and obstructed the line of vision. The object, remaining close to the eyes, was in continual movement. At times, it jerked right or left, and other times, it shook. And then, as quickly as it appeared, what looked like a tiny fist disappeared. The high tops reappeared, and a greasy taste of baby oil filled Bella's mouth. She spit and spit some more, but her taste buds were well-oiled.

A sharp noise poked against her eardrum and prison bars filled the line of vision as the infant searched for the source of the noise. Again, a sharp, high-pitched noise struck the ear. As it drew closer, words filtered through. "Sammy? Is Mama's little girl awake?" Bella felt the warmth, comfort, and security on both sides of her back. The prison bars disappeared and were replaced by tiny animal figures hanging from strings that moved in a circle. And a bright light, in the center of the parade of animals, was blinding.

Without immediately acknowledging it, her nose wrinkled and relaxed, wrinkled and relaxed. The wrinkling shielded her from an offensive mingling of aromas while relaxing invited the smells to drift upward. One aroma was sweet and light, and the other was foul and heavy. The mixing of the two made her stomach roll. The voice who identified herself as Mama was the source of the sweet smell and the source that named the foul odor. "Did Mama's little girl go poopy?" Perfume and poop, not a pleasant blend.

Beholding the face of Mama, less than three inches from her face, Bella understood that she was experiencing reality through the senses of the infant. She saw reality, heard reality, smelt it, touched it, and tasted it through the senses of the baby.

The baby had a story to share. How wrong she had been! How naïve to assume that the story of life only begins at the moment one remembers, or more accurately, the moment one can call it forth.

Her cheek grew wet and warm, and Bella nodded with understanding. She even raised her hand and touched the spot on her face.

Although there was no wetness, she knew, she knew that was where Mama kissed her baby.

The space grew dark. The light that cast shadows of tiny animals circling the room faded. The only sound was the rhythm of breath, taken in and pushed out, taken in and pushed out. Freshness, like that of an April sunrise after a night of rain, filled the nose. The lingering presence of sweet milk coated the tongue. Yet darkness ruled and Bella was forced to wait.

In the darkness, not of the room, not of sleep, but of the absence of breath, Bella experienced what the infant did not. She heard what the child would never hear; a woman shrieking. She felt the warmth, first of hands and then Mama's body. A touch, the child would never feel. Her cheeks were bathed in wetness that, when it reached her mouth, was salty. A brackishness the child would never taste. Bella smelled for the very first time what her mom described as the smell of death. A smell the child's mama would never forget.

In the darkness, Bella saw others begin to arrive in the room. One of them took the infant from her mother's arms and carefully returned the child to the crib while others engulfed mama with hugs and kisses and shared the wetness on their cheeks. As they ushered Mama from the room, one of them, an older woman, who had similar features to Mama, but was hunched over as she stood, stopped at the side of the prison bars, reached down, and carefully removed the purple high tops with faux fur and rubber soles made from the milk of the Hevea tree.

Bella could not stand it anymore. She kicked the purple shoes from her feet and pushed her body away from the floor to flee the dressing room. Standing on the other side of the sheet, she was aware that her breath was shallow and quick. All of her senses were slowly returning to "normal." Normal, she wondered. What is normal?

Is it normal for an infant should die during an afternoon nap? Is it normal that a mama will never again hold her own flesh and blood? Is it normal that purple high tops with faux fur should be brought to a second-hand store? Is it normal that she should feel the need to make this right?

Retrieving her Doc Martens from the dressing room with one hand, she used the other to carry the purple high tops out into the light of the store. The illumination confirmed the task that awaited her.

Two quarters held four wrinkled dollar bills in place next to the cash register as Bella switched off the last light in the Rerun Thrift Store and pulled the door shut.

Chapter 9

She pulled her phone from her back right pocket as she walked briskly down the sidewalk. A slight tap of the screen brought the phone to life and the numbers near the top read 12:23 PM. There was no hope. She was going to be late for work. The events of the morning took much longer than she planned. She was awake and out of bed by 7:30. If only she had gotten up an hour earlier.

By 12:42 she stood in the hallway of an apartment building. The number on the door in front of her was 112. Carefully cradled under her arm was the pair of purple high tops. For the first time since she started working for Marge, she was happy that Marge required the collection of information from individuals who donated items. Since the shoes had just arrived at the store, the paperwork had yet to be filed, making it easier for Bella to locate the address before she left the store the night before.

What consumed the majority of her morning was what Bella possessed in her left hand. It was a single piece of paper. It was not the collection of the paper that took time but the writing and rewriting of the words the paper held. Bella wanted the message to be clear yet offering a glimmer of hope for the future. The message read:

You may not want these now, too many memories. But someday, these

>   *memories will bring you peace and joy. Keep them close to your heart.*

She carefully placed the purple high tops in front of the door with the note rolled up and placed in the shoe. She knocked forcefully, her knuckles immediately reddened, and she took off running.

Her lungs fought for air and her chest burned, but her feet refused to stop as they pounded the concrete. The Doc Martens sounded like the hooves of buffalo on the prairie. Thump, thump, thump. Three blocks from the apartment building, she stopped abruptly and pushed her face into a lilac bush where the contents of her stomach clung to the branches. The sleeve of her shirt served as a towel to wipe her mouth and dab the sweat from her forehead. She fished a stick of gum from the front pocket of her jeans as she regained her balance and proceeded to walk beyond the sight of the twelve-story apartment building.

A block and a half later, she pulled her phone out, it read, 12:51. "Shit." She looked about to see if anyone heard her. She had to be at work by 1, and the store was across town.

Chapter 10

Bella stepped through the doorway and was greeted by a hint of cool air. The contrast between the heat of the afternoon sun coupled with her run-walk effort to cover the city blocks in record time, and the cool air of the store resulted in an involuntary shiver. The initial shiver was accompanied by a second as Bella was also greeted by Marge, less than three feet from the front door.

"Good afternoon, Bella. Late night?"

Bella tried to surmise what Marge was implying by "late night." Was this a question regarding the time of her departure from the store, or inquiring about any behavior after leaving work? Bella decided a short and simple response would cover both. "No."

For a few brief seconds, Bella thought her response was sufficient as she moved past her employer and didn't hear any objections. But then…

"Oh, Bella."

She stopped but didn't turn to face Marge as she said "Yes?"

"Did anyone come to the store last night after closing?"

Slowly, Bella turned and looked directly at Marge. Her forehead was wrinkled as her reply was merely a repeat of Marge's question, "Anyone come to the store?"

"Yes. I was surprised to discover four dollars and fifty cents next to the cash register, which I am sure was not there last night when I left. My first thought was someone came to the door after I left, you let them in, and they made a purchase."

"No, no one came to the door last night."

"Do you have any idea where that money came from?"

Unable to look at Marge, Belle turned and started to walk away as she answered. "Nope. No idea."

Before Bella could reach the breakroom and start to breathe again, Marge stopped her yet again with another question. "Belle, I also noticed that the pair of baby shoes are not on the rack. Did you clean them and place them on the rack last night?"

She knew she had to turn around and face Marge. As she did, she realized that a fellow employee in the Rerun Thrift Store was staring directly at her. It was in the air and she too sensed that something significant was unfolding between her and Marge.

She answered honestly, but not truthfully, and her voice was weak and quivered, despite trying to speak with confidence. "Yes, I cleaned them and placed them on the rack after I mopped and cleaned the bathroom."

Marge smiled. It was the smile Bella has witnessed countless times from her mother. It was the same smile that Ralphie in the movie *A Christmas Story* received from his father after being asked if he, Ralphie, had been good. Marge wasn't her mother or Santa, yet that smile told Bella that Marge knew. The question was just how much did Marge know?

As she walked into the breakroom, she felt the eyes of her fellow employee still gazing at her back. She could feel the disappointment in the air as her breathing patterns gained some level of normalcy. Obviously she had hoped that Marge would do more than smile. She hoped she might see a side of Marge seldom witnessed. A side that would yell and possibly even fire someone for arriving late to work. But that wasn't Marge. Bella knew that for sure. What she didn't know was *who is Marge?*

Chapter 11

Temperatures that usually didn't arrive until July had been the mainstay the entire month of June. Nearly everyone who entered the Rerun Thrift Store started every conversation with the same five words, "Can you believe the weather?" The hope that the weather pattern might reverse itself so July would bring June temperatures was simply that, hope. A hope and desire that did not materialize as the temperatures crept even higher. Taxing everyone's cooling units and temperaments.

Bella continued to pick up the closing shift at work, but she avoided the shoes on the north wall. She needed an emotional break from witnessing the lives of the people who owned the shoes. She also needed to step back and take stock of Marge. Marge had always treated her well. She treated everyone with respect, but…there was just something she could not identify that told her there was more about Marge than anyone had witnessed.

Earlier in the week, Marge's action left everyone scraping their chins off the wooden floor. Marge, with the business's phone in hand, punched only three times on the keypad, waited, and then said, "Police, I wish to report a theft at the Rerun Thrift Store."

The words vibrated through the store, "Theft? What was stolen?" Or more accurately, what was stolen of enough value that would cause Marge to phone the police? Shoplifting was something all employees were trained to watch for, but the police were never called. Employees would report the act to Marge and she would handle the situation with the individual.

A police officer arrived and followed Marge into her overcrowded office. There was barely enough floor space available for a chair. As a result the officer elected to stand.

The employees huddled in small pods and tried to figure out what was happening. What has been taken and who had stolen something valuable enough to have the police in the store?

The door opened and Marge stepped out. Behind her body, one could see that a lone chair sat in front of Marge's desk and the officer stood off to the side with notepads open and pen in hand. Marge scanned the room, clearly searching for one individual in particular. Was it a customer or an employee? It could hardly be an employee. Who would ever think of stealing from Marge?

Spotting the person, Marge walked across the floor of the Rerun Thrift Store and in whispering tones spoke with Ronald. He nodded his head as he listened to Marge speak and then both of them returned to her office. Before the door was shut, everyone watched as Ronald lowered his body into the waiting chair.

The pods of conversation erupted again with consensus that Ronald, the store manager, must have information critical to the investigation. The number of people in the store increased over the next twenty minutes, as no one left and additional customers entered. Within a matter of minutes, new arrivals were informed of the situation unfolding behind the door. The door that held everyone's attention.

When the door finally opened, the officer exited followed by Ronald, who was in handcuffs. The two silently made their way across the store and departed the building without Ronald making eye contact with anyone.

The moment the front door closed the room exploded. No one tried to conceal their excitement at what they just witnessed. Rumors flew from one corner of the building to another.

"I always knew he couldn't be trusted."

"He had that look about him."

"I wonder what it was that he did. It had to be big."

"If I had to guess, I would say…"

The moment Marge stepped from her office, the entire room fell silent. She held up her hand in front of her and patted the air. She looked worn, even defeated. Before she spoke, she stepped over to the nearest rack of clothes and took hold of the top spindle. There she gained her balance. She stared at the floor for several seconds, and then scanned the room. Looking directly into the face of every person in the room, she said, "You know, a person is innocent until proven guilty. And therefore, I would never say anything until a thorough investigation has occurred and if necessary, a court case has been concluded."

After a brief pause to clear her throat, Marge continued, "However, the situation before us today is slightly different. It is different because Ronald has confessed to the crime committed. I wish I could say it was simply petty theft, and we could handle the situation in-house. Unfortunately, it is more serious than that. I will not give any specifics, nor will I speculate about what will happen to Ronald. As I already stated, it is serious. If there is anything positive about today's events, it is that a huge burden, a burden built on endless lies and deception, has been lifted from Ronald. There is no excuse for what he did, but at least now the healing can start. This is the last time we will speak of this issue. Thank you. People, let's get back to work and others, please, shop."

Bella desperately wanted to follow Marge into her office and sit and listen. She didn't need the details that would eventually appear in the newspaper of how Ronald embezzled more than thirty thousand dollars from a secondhand store over the years. She wanted to understand how could Marge be so forgiving. Ronald, a man whom Marge trusted, just made a mockery of everything she stood for and her primary concern was for him and the process of healing.

Three days after what became known as "the event," Marge informed Bella that several pairs of shoes had come in during the past week and she wanted them sanitized and placed on the rack. When Bella asked if she should do the task immediately, Marge said she could complete the task after mopping and cleaning the toilets.

Surprised by Marge's response, Bella said, "But I don't close tonight. I'm only scheduled until six."

"Yes, I know. Ronald was scheduled to close, but well… I assumed you would be willing to cover." There was no question asking if she could or would consider closing, just the expectation that she would.

Hesitating, Bella said, "Yeah, I suppose I can stay and close. I don't have any plans for the evening. I will take care of the shoes as well."

The store had been busier than usual the entire evening, especially the bathroom. The tiny bathroom had been occupied with a steady stream of visitors starting earlier than most nights and continuing until Bella locked the door well past closing time. As a result, it was after eleven before Bella picked up the first pair of shoes.

The length of her forearm, nearly up to her elbow, was consumed by the boot as she reached in to make sure nothing was wedged in the narrow toe. Cowboy boots were not an item that appeared frequently on the north wall of the store. When a pair did arrive, they would remain for months; it was not like many cowboys came shopping for a pair of boots in a secondhand store. The exception was the month of October. Customers from across town, in search of the authentic Halloween costume, would snatch them up immediately with little regard to the actual size or condition.

Cowboy boots fascinated Bella. She had never owned a pair, and other than a few mavericks in school, she didn't know anyone brave or stupid enough to wear a pair. But that was not what captured her interest. It was the practical and formal design that gave her pause as she sterilized the boots. The boots could be worn for work. Worn when riding a horse, branding cattle, mending fences, pitching manure, or climbing on the back of a bull. That was something she had seen once or twice on TV and couldn't understand why anyone with even a sliver of common sense would attempt to ride a two-thousand-pound animal. An animal that was as powerful and agile as any beast. The same pair of boots with a quick swipe of a damp cloth or even a little boot polish and spit would serve well for a social outing. Worn for shopping, dining out, dancing, even going to church. The rugged design and craftsmanship that lasted for years, coupled with the preparation of the leather and stitching for aesthetic appearances provided a cowboy footwear for any occasion. The pair before her on the workbench was no exception.

The pristine condition of the tri-colored boots led Bella to conclude that the boots had not seen the labors of chores or even the sides of a horse. There were no scuff marks dug into the snakeskin that covered the pointed tips of the toe. No creases in the leather vamp across the top of the boot from endless use. The leather soles and heels were not worn down to the right or left. The craving on the leather high tops that protected the shin and calf from branches and sage brush on the trail did not carry dust and dirt. Even the dye imprint of the name brand stamped on the inside of the boot was not faded from sweat. These boots belonged to a man who wore them only for social outings or did not have an opportunity to wear them for work. The question that stirred as Bella carried the boots to the north wall was did these boots belong to a real cowboy or just a wannabe?

The boots never found their place on the wall before Bella carried them into the dressing room and hooked her index fingers through the leather pull straps at the top of the boot. Her foot traveled downward with little effort until it rested firmly on the welt of the boot. She was surprised how comfortable the boots were. Rather than looking at the mirror, she stepped past the sheet and walked across the store. The hollow sound of the boots striking the floor was mesmerizing. The sound became a mantra of sorts, thump, thump, thump, and her concentration heightened. She became aware of her entire body moving, every muscle at work making the movement possible. But the longer she walked, the more haunting the sound grew. It was as though the boots were mocking her, asking the question with every footfall, *What - if? What - if? What - if?*

Pulling back the sheet, seeing the same boots in the mirror, twice their actual size, striking a wooden floor and a male figure within the boots, Bella understood this was not her question. It belonged to the owner of the boots. "What – if? What – if?"

Bella whispered, "What – if, what?" as though she expected an answer to appear. When none did, she took her now traditional seat across from the mirror and watched. She watched a man walk without ever going anywhere. It was like he was on a treadmill, walking but not really moving. But there was no treadmill. The volume increased and the hollow sound of the boot filled the room, *what – if?*

Bella addressed the mirror, equal in volume to the thump, with an edge to her question, "What – if, what?"

All she heard was thump, thump, *What – if? What – if?*, and she allowed herself to be pulled in deeper and deeper by the mantra. The more she relaxed the more she saw. The more she understood. The more she became one with the man. A man who looked like a cowboy. A man whose name was Cody.

This was the last pair of boots Cody would purchase. He was well aware of that fact the moment he threw the cash on the counter. He was all too aware of that fact, even though at that moment evidence was not yet available to prove the fact. Such evidence would not be available for another three years.

This, his last pair of boots, did not serve any of the practical purposes previous boots had. Another fact he acknowledged the moment the cash was pulled from his wallet. He could no longer mend fences or pitch manure, bull riding had not happened in decades, and getting on the back of a horse was next to impossible. The sole purpose of this pair of boots was to carry his body and help him recall the days when he could do all those things.

Recollection of days gone by took him to a day he stood before the proverbial fork in the road. His choice of footwear that memorable day had been a pair of cowboy boots too.

His father, early one the morning while preparing to leave the house, announced that he would be out checking the cattle. When he didn't return late in the afternoon, the hired men saddled their horse and went out to find him. An hour into the search, his horse was spotted and there next to the horse lay his father. The doctor said his heart exploded. When Cody arrived home the next day, he wasn't completely sure what that meant, other than there was nothing anyone could have done, even if his father had been in the hospital.

Cody was two months into his senior year of college, already accepted into a medical program at the university. He desired to become a medical doctor. He wanted to work with people, to eventually specialize in oncology. His goal was to one day develop a new life-saving treatment for cancer.

Thump, thump, thump, thump. The volume again increased. *What – if? What – if?*

The fork in the road leaped out and pulled him forward. Should he selfishly pursue his desires and his dreams, or should he return home and take over the ranch?

Seated at the dining room table, he was surrounded by his mother, his uncle and aunt who ranched with his dad, and his girlfriend, soon-to-be fiancé, or so he hoped. His girlfriend, a city girl, had experienced horses and cows up close for the first time when she came home with Cody a year earlier. They had dated off and on over the past two years but became inseparable during the course of the past year. The struggle became real as he felt a sense of loyalty and responsibility to everyone at the table, for everyone except himself.

He pushed his chair back slightly from the oak table and folded his hands in his lap. It was at that moment that he realized the answer stared him in the face. He had been back in the house less than twenty-four hours, and the loafers he wore every day had been replaced by a pair of cowboy boots. His future was not loafers or rubber sole shoes that squeaked on a sterile floor. His future was leather cowboy boots.

Thump. The decision cost him his girlfriend. Thump. The decision faded any dream of becoming a doctor. Thump. The decision carried with it an unanswerable question "What – if?" that haunted him with every step he took.

So he rose early the next morning, and just like his father, he announced, as he prepared to leave the house, that he was going to check the cattle. For the next sixty years, he rose each morning to mend fences, pitch manure, doctor cattle and horses, and live the life that others could only dream about. He was a cowboy.

A cowboy who understood horses better than people.

A cowboy, with time to think on horseback while searching for
a stray calf, was a philosopher.

A cowboy who buried his mother, uncle, and aunt, and was left
to rattle about in a two-story five-bedroom house.

A cowboy who saw no purpose or value in TV and read a book from cover to cover every three days.

A cowboy who despised guns and kept a loaded shotgun next to the front door to shoot predators that threatened his livestock. Or carried rabies.

A cowboy who welcomed a shot of whiskey, a cold beer, and a dry wine.

A cowboy who drank his coffee black as coal and as thick as molasses.

A cowboy who went to town once a month.

A cowboy who would drive 50 miles across the countryside rather than pick up a phone.

A cowboy whose boots echoed on the wooden floor with each step he took and...

"A cowboy," Bella said. "A real cowboy. A cowboy who didn't merely wear boots but lived boots."

Chapter 12

Bella abandoned the dressing room, leaving the cowboy in the mirror still walking but not making any progress. She stood tall as she strolled about the store and passed the elevated desk and swivel bar stool with a backrest that previously was controlled by Ronald. The desk was a concoction that Ronald created to give him a greater sense of authority and importance. A wooden dictionary stand appeared in the store shortly after he was hired, which he abruptly confiscated and removed from the store. Three days later the top portion of the wooden stand returned to the store having been attached to a small round wooden three-foot-high end-table. The newly designed "desk" as Ronald called it stood four and a half feet high. Behind the desk, Ronald took his perch each day. With papers on the stand and a coffee cup tittering on the edge of the cluttered round table, Ronald would bark out orders to the employees. Or at least until Marge would pass by his desk of authority and softly whisper, "You catch more flies with honey than with vinegar."

She hadn't noticed it the first time she passed Ronald's now clean workspace, but on a return passage, Bella couldn't ignore the thump from the boots on the floor.

Thump, Thump. It sounded the same as the question haunting Cody, the cowboy. *What – if?*

Bella stopped and leaned against the desk. Could it be? Was Ronald's life, like Cody's, defined by an endless search for an answer to what if? Could Ronald's theft be explained by his inability to make peace with himself?

It took Bella several strides to reach the dressing room and retrieve her Doc Martens. With each step, the sound grew louder. Thump, thump, *thump, THUMP. What – if? What – if?*

* * *

Bella stood before a uniformed county officer attempting to answer a battery of questions to the best of her ability. After answering the usual questions related to identity and confirming that identity with documentation, the officer, who appeared only a few years older than Bella, inquired, "What is the purpose of your visit with Ronald Harrison?"

Surprised by the question, Bella stumbled for a politically correct answer, "Uhm, well, I… I ah… I want to speak with him."

"About what?"

Suspicious and annoyed with this line of questions, Bella sharpened her response. "I don't see how that is any of your business."

"Well, you do understand, young lady, we are dealing here with a state prisoner who is merely being held in custody in the county jail until space is available to transport him to the state prison."

Young lady? Who does this pimple face kid think he is? He pulls on a tan uniform and carries a plastic taser, and he becomes god?

Bella was smart enough to know, if she had any hope of speaking with Ronald, being a smartass wouldn't secure that objective. She cleared her throat and proceeded in hopes of convincing the power-hungry officer that she wasn't a threat to the security of the jail or providing Ronald with contraband he might use to escape.

"I worked with Ronald in a secondhand store in the neighboring town called the Rerun Thrift Store. Ronald…"

The officer, holding his clipboard with all the vital information from his interrogation of Bella, interrupted her in mid-sentence. "Hey, I know that store. I was there a few years ago looking for a Halloween costume."

"As I was saying, Ronald was my manager at the store. He was always nice to me, and I wanted to return the favor before he was shipped off to the state prison, where I'm pretty sure I would never get in to see him. That's all."

"I suppose there's nothing too dangerous about that. Hey, you still working at that thrift store?"

"Yes, I am."

"Maybe, I'll have to swing by there some time and check out the goods."

My God, the creep is hitting on me. Bella knew she was close to seeing Ronald. *Just respond professionally.*

"If you do stop by, come in the morning. That way you can pick through all the good stuff before others get a chance to buy it." *Plus, I never work in the morning.*

Bella was ushered into a windowless room that held several tables eight to ten feet apart. On both ends of the room stood an officer in a tan uniform. Unlike the deputy who questioned her, these men had real guns on their hips. She realized at that moment that she really had not thought this part of the visit through. She had envisioned standing outside the bars speaking with Ronald as he sat on his cot. She smiled as she shook her head. Too many cop shows.

Ronald arrived in handcuffs and was cuffed to the table once seated. He didn't say anything, but the expression on his face spoke volumes. He just stared at her as his face grew wet with tears.

Bella, unsure where to start, finally said, "Hi, Ronald."

"Ron."

"What?"

"Call me Ron."

"Okay. Hi Ron."

The tears were now accompanied by shoulders shaking. The edge of the table in front of Ron was developing a pool of tears as he kept his head tilted forward. The man was sobbing. Bella wasn't prepared for this. She expected to speak with the man who ordered people around. A voice that was always gruff and never included a hint of compassion. She was at a complete loss for what to say. She simply sat there and watched and waited. It felt as though she was on the floor in the dressing room at the thrift store staring into the mirror.

Ron lifted his head but avoided eye contact. "I'm sorry."

"No need to..." She stopped herself, and started again, "Sorry? Sorry for what?" It always disturbed her that another person's uncomfortableness would silence her whenever she was vulnerable and shared her feelings. She would not permit herself to do the same to Ron.

"I'm just sorry."

There had to be more, but she didn't respond. It was just like the mirror. When the character whose shoes she wore was ready to share their story, they would. Until then, it was her job to wait.

"Why are you here, Bella? What do you want from me?"

"Do I have to want something from you in order to be here?"

"Doesn't everyone want something?"

"What do you want, Ron?"

"I want..." he stopped and leaned back in the metal folding chair. He looked directly at her for a long period without speaking. Without changing his body position, he started again. "I want to go back and start again. I want to live a different life."

The thought screamed in her head; this was Cody's question. The only difference was Ron had declared he wanted to take the other road.

Ron crossed his legs under the table and said, "You are the only person who has come to visit me. I really want to know, why did you come?"

"Because I met a man once, a cowboy, who lived his entire life trying to answer the question, 'what if?,' and I wanted to know if that was true for you as well."

"Does that mean you want to know why I embezzled the money?"

"Not unless it's important for you to tell me."

He sat there for a moment, staring past her, looking back into the past, his past. And then, he shook his head. "No, no, it's not important, because anything I say would sound like an excuse. There is no excuse."

"Is it too late for you to live a different life?"

"I don't know," Ron answered without a moment's hesitation and then he leaned forward, narrowing the distance between himself and Bella. The two officers noticed and directed their full attention to Ron. In a soft voice, with a hint of compassion, he inquired, "Was it too late for your cowboy friend? Did he ever answer the question?"

"I don't know. He hasn't told me the end of his story yet."

"When he does, will you come back and let me know what he said?"

Chapter 13

Cody's tri-colored cowboy boots

The old man in the mirror who walked and appeared to never make any progress stopped quite unexpectedly. The frail body, showing the effects of hard labor, bobbed back and forth ever so slightly as though it had grown accustomed to constant movement that it wasn't sure how to respond to stillness. The body turned and Bella watched as the old cowboy with his legs bowed and a hitch in his right hip climbed the stairs.

Cody entered a room that was obviously his bedroom and slowly lowered himself to sit on the edge of the bed. The task that followed took nearly ten minutes, but he finally succeeded in removing the tri-colored boots from his feet. Exhausted from the task that at times contorted his body, he rested for several more minutes breathing deeply and wishing, willing the oxygen to feed his muscles and make him strong once again.

With one final cleansing breath in and out, Cody pushed himself off the bed and shuffled across the floor to a closet door. Lowering himself down to his hands and knees, the old man crowded to the back wall of the closet to gather up a pair of shoes that had been buried beneath bags of junk. Before returning to the bed with the shoes in hand, he stopped at the chest of a drawer and picked up a small tin of shoe polish and a cotton rag. Seated on the edge of the bed he applied layer after layer to the shoes, first rubbing it in and then buffing it off.

With the loafers polished and perfectly placed next to the side of the bed, Cody, with little effort, slid his feet into the shoes. He stood and admired the results of his labor. He completed three laps about the bedroom, stopping from time to time to look down at the shoes. Seated once more on the edge of the bed, he kicked off the loafers and watched as they landed in the middle of the room. He sat there and just stared at the finely polished loafers he had not placed on his feet for more than sixty years.

He then bent over, picked up first the right boot, placed his index fingers in the leather straps, and pulled with all his might until his foot reached the bottom. The left boot followed in turn. He leaned back upon the bed, and with as much effort as he could muster, he hoisted his legs upon the bed and placed his head on the pillow. He closed his eyes, and a simple smile creased his lips.

Chapter 14

She knew it was him the moment he walked through the front door. Even if she hadn't seen his face, she would have identified him by his gait. It was difficult to explain how she knew. He stepped with power and yet grace, with authority and yet kindness. She knew she could never describe a gait of kindness; one just had to experience it.

Although she had seen him, she wasn't sure he had seen her. Therefore, she moved with a degree of urgency and placed herself in the middle of women's clothing. She searched the floor in the hope of finding clothing that had fallen off hangers that would provide a reason, an excuse why she was not visible about the rack of clothes. Her desperate efforts to hide herself from the gentleman who entered the store ended as Marge stood next to her kneeling body.

"Bella, there is a young gentleman, one I believe you know, who clearly needs some assistance."

Before Bella could object or even rise and let her facial expression speak her discomfort with that directive, Marge was gone.

Slowly Bella exited the aisle of women's plus size clothing and crossed to the other side of the store where Brent stood staring at a tub filled with gloves.

"Kind of early to be shopping for winter gloves." Bella tried to be witty as a way to cover her nervousness.

"Gloves? Oh, yeah, gloves. No, I don't need gloves. I really don't need anything, I was sort of… well, you know… hoping that you were working."

"Well, as you can see, I am. Now that we have that settled, I will leave you to your not needing to shop so I can get back to work." Bella immediately turned and walked back to the women's section.

"Wait, Bella. I really want to talk to you. How late do you work tonight?"

She stopped and walked back toward Brent. As she did, she thought about lying but instead told the truth. "I am off at six."

"Is it okay if I give you a ride home?"

She thought for a moment and then said, "I don't know. Are there any plans to stop off at any lakes."

"Lakes?" Brent's facial expression revealed that he didn't understand.

"You know, watching the sun come up!" The words dripped with sarcasm.

Brent took a half step back from her before he spoke, "Oh, yeah. No. I promise, no lakes."

"Well... I suppose... since there will be no trip to a lake, you can drive me home."

She watched Brent walk out of the store and his gait was more grace and kindness than power and authority, and she wondered if something happened over the summer that changed him. She also realized that, despite her initial nervousness, it was easy to talk with him. How quickly she permitted herself to be herself with him, again.

The hours could not tick by quickly enough to end her shift so that she might see him again. Even Marge commented.

"Bella, you are fluttering around the store today like a butterfly. What's the deal?"

Bella just shrugged her shoulders and fluttered away.

Brent stepped into the store fifteen minutes before six. Marge smiled and asked Bella if her chariot arrived.

Bella tilted her head and asked, "How'd you know?"

"One would need to be blind not to see how the two of you affect the other."

That comment gave Bella pause. She had not considered that she might have an effect on Brent in the same way he affected her. She also realized, yet again, that Marge seemed to have a knack for seeing things others did not and for helping her see life more clearly.

* * *

They drove through the city streets in silence as song after song filtered through the speakers. Which was okay with Bella. It allowed her to smell him again without being distracted by having to make conversation. His scent was pleasing, enticing, even desirable. Until that moment, less than two feet from his side, she had forgotten just how much she loved the aroma that his body emitted.

She had even researched, when they were still dating, how scents can attract people to one another. The chemical compatibility argument was made in article after article suggesting that the human scent can bring some people together. It made her smile as she fully acknowledged that the factors resulting in compatibility between people were greater than smell, but that did not change the fact that she liked Brent's natural musky scent.

The thought of articles about scent faded the moment Brent asked if she was hungry and would like to stop and get something to eat. He suggested picking up some fast food and stopping at the city park.

Not having eaten since breakfast, Bella was quick to respond. "Yeah." Still admiring his profile, she added, "Let me text my mom so she doesn't wait for me and try and keep supper warm."

With a bag in hand, holding their burgers and fries, Brent directed Bella to select where in the park she would like to sit as they ate.

His request surprised her. It seemed like he was being overly cautious. Like he didn't want to risk his actions being misinterpreted.

Bella nodded and, with their drinks in both hands, quickly set off in search of a picnic table beyond earshot of the crowd that sought comfort from an evening breeze, yet not out of sight of others.

The two exchanged brief interludes of eye contact quite like what one might expect to witness with young adolescents on a first date, or a divorced couple encountering each other for the first time in public.

Bella decided that since Brent initiated this… she wasn't sure what to call it. It certainly wasn't a date, or was it? A rendezvous? An appointment? A rendezvous sounded sinister and an appointment too cold and sterile. She had always wanted to use the word tryst to describe an action, but… that only made her think about the lake. Probably the best word to describe this event was the boring word *meeting*. Since Brent initiated this meeting, it was up to him to set the agenda, or at least propose one.

In between bites of his cheeseburger, which also held a thin slice of bacon, Brent stuttered several times before the words, "I'm sorry" were audible. Without looking up he had delivered the apology. He then quickly shoved three French fries into his mouth.

Reaching across the picnic table, placing her fingers under his chin, and lifting his head until their eyes met, Bella asked, "Sorry for what?"

After a deep breath and time to swallow the fries, he said, "I am sorry for the way I treated you. No, for the way I disrespected you last spring. I want to share with you who I was back then, not to justify my actions, but… well, I want you to know that I am now working to become someone different. I also, if possible, would like you to meet this new person I am working to become."

Bella considered what she had just heard. The pain from last spring was still raw, still hurt. She had allowed herself to be so vulnerable, so honest, so… herself. She didn't know if she could permit that again with Brent. Without realizing it, she had pushed back from the table and therefore when she lowered her eyes, she noticed that Brent was wearing flip-flops. The image of George flashed before her eyes. The color drained from her face to the point that Brent asked, "Bella, are you okay?"

Looking at Brent and then again at the flip-flops, she answered. "I need a minute to take all this in. I need… I need to stand up and move, to walk."

Brent rose with her.

Both her hands rose as though she were surrendering, but in reality she was pushing Brent back. "No. Please wait. Give me a moment. I need to walk by myself. Trust me. I am not leaving. I just need a minute."

Brent returned to the bench of the picnic table while Bella turned and walked off. She moved further away from the crowd and into the solitude of the park.

Stepping off the narrow path, Bella lowered herself to the trunk of a fallen tree. Her hands cradled her head which was throbbing. What just happened? She asked herself several times. Never outside of the dressing room had she seen the image of a character so clearly. George, with his flip-flops, leaned forward to pull another cigarette from the box, even though the one in his mouth was not yet finished. What did this mean?

Bella lifted her head and searched the sky above at the sound of chatter. Two baby squirrels were chasing one another, leaping from tree limb to tree limb and then from branch to branch. At times, their weight was greater than the strength of the branch and the branch would dip toward the ground, dropping three or four feet, but the squirrels hung on and rode it out, waiting for the opportunity to leap to the next branch, hoping it would be more secure.

Perhaps that was the answer. She, too, needed to hang on and ride it out. The branch hadn't snapped, nor was there any evidence it was about to. She needed to listen to whatever Brent wanted or needed to share. Just as she patiently waited for each character to share their story. She needed to be patient and let Brent's story unfold as he saw fit. The only problem was that it was so much easier to sit idle when wearing their shoes.

Before she left the log and returned to the path, Bella confessed to herself that she was not ready to put on Brent's shoes and feel his story, nor was she ready to let him wear hers.

Seated across from him again, she thanked him for the moment of solitude and added, "Please, tell me what it is you want me to know."

"Do you know where I spent the summer?"

"Not specifically. I assumed you were attending different athletic camps. Camps for football and wrestling."

With a partial smile, he said, "That's what everyone was supposed to think."

"Where did you spend the summer?" Interest in the answer to the question dripped from every word.

"I don't know if you knew, but I got pretty banged up during the state championship football game. I spent Sunday in the hospital with some minor internal injuries and a hamstring injury that just refused to heal. Anyway, because my body was basically one massive bruise, the doctor discharged me with some painkillers."

Cautiously, Bella asked, "You mean like opioids, Oxycontin or Vicodin.?"

"Exactly. The prescription was for Vicodin. I have to admit it worked. It worked so well that by the time wrestling season started, I needed the pills to get me through practice. And then to get me through school."

"I didn't know. I mean… I never suspected." As though she was in a dark room watching a photo come to life, she stopped for a moment and permitted the photo to become clearer. And when it came into focus, she reached across the table, grabbed his hand, and said, "Oh, my God, Brent, you were taking these and drinking on top of that."

"You weren't supposed to know. And unfortunately, I was good at hiding it from everyone. Until…" Brent reached for her other hand before he continued. "Until prom. By the time we reached the lake I was so high, spinning back and forth between the drugs and the alcohol that I had no filter. No thought processes." He stopped and shrugged his shoulders and shook his head. There was no way to explain his behavior.

Holding each other's hand, they sat in silence and studied every feature of the other's face. They both would have humbled any challengers in a blinking contest. Without breaking his gaze, Brent moved forward with his account.

"I couldn't live with myself for the way I treated you and then when you… well, it's not your fault. I don't know how I finished the school year. I literally don't remember anything about school other than trying to talk with and… failing. I wasn't only failing; I was a failure. I couldn't go on. I…"

"Are you saying that you tried to kill yourself?"

"Yeah, I tried several times. Fortunately, the last time, my brother was home, or I would not be sitting here talking to you right now."

"I didn't try to end my life because you didn't talk to me, but because I was in such a dark place and I didn't know how to get out. The drug took control of my every waking moment. I used you to try and convince myself that I was anchored, that I could handle and control my drug use."

"And when I pushed back, you…"

"My entire world crumbled down upon me. It's so ironic."

Bella tilted her head slightly and asked, "What's ironic?"

"The drug was supposed to permit me to be a part of reality, a part of life, when all it was doing was slowly distorting reality and silencing my life."

Brent could no longer look directly at Bella. He stared at the top of the picnic table layered with grime from the elements and food. It was only with Bella's prompting that Brent spoke of his summer.

"So you didn't attend any sports camps. Where did you spend the summer?"

"It was my brother's connections through his job with the government…"

"Secret service?"

"Close enough. He was able to pull strings and get me into a drug rehab. facility within twelve hours. I went directly from the hospital to rehab."

"Hospital?"

"Yeah, they had to pump my stomach and monitor my vitals to make sure my body didn't shut down. I found out later that the doctors said the only reason I survived was because I was in such good physical shape. Otherwise, I should be dead. During my program, I told myself and therapists, 'I survived because I need to make things right with you.'"

Bella blushed. It was her turn to stare at the tabletop.

Recognizing that she was questioning his final confession, he added, "I'm serious, Bella. You mean so much to me that I needed to tell you the truth."

Looking up, she said, "I believe you."

The sun dropped behind the trees and darkness drifted across the park, and they found themselves alone in the park.

Bella asked, "So, now what?"

Brent let go of her hands and climbed out from between the tabletop and the bench seat. He stood staring down at her. "I... I don't... know. I never really thought beyond telling you the truth."

Looking up at him she pressed on. "What do you want?"

He smiled and allowed himself to look off into the distance. "Sorry, I'm smiling because I was thinking about the last time I heard that question. It forced me to be honest with myself, just as you are requesting at this moment."

"I guess I am."

"It's really hard to answer that because it makes me sound so selfish."

"Yet when you were high, it didn't bother you to be selfish."

"I guess not. I never thought of it that way."

"Don't you believe you have the right to ask for what you want?"

Brent returned to the bench and asked, "Do you?"

"I didn't. But several experiences have taught me that it's okay to be honest and state what you need. Besides, life is too short and goes by too quickly not to! So, you're up."

"Bella, I really like you, I want to spend time with you, and I want you, if you agree, to get to know me as I am now. I want to start dating you again."

Bella continued to look directly at him and nodded her head several times to acknowledge that she understood what he wanted. But for the moment, words were not available.

Unsure what the silence meant, Brent spoke, "I can take you home if you want."

"Want?" Even though it was dark, the entire park was only lit by a single light in the parking lot some three hundred yards away, her eyes were visible. "Brent, I was waiting for you to ask me what I wanted."

"I thought I made that clear when I said, 'If you agree.'"

"No, you were asking if I agreed with what you wanted. That's not asking me what I want."

"I'm sorry. Bella, tell me, really, I want to know. What do you want?"

She didn't need to pause, and she spoke with some urgency. "I want a relationship that is safe, secure, and trustworthy. I want someone who wants me for me and not to change me or make me fit some dream. Brent, I also want to spend time with you. I want to start dating you too, but you need to promise me that you will always be open and honest with me. You need to promise that you will help me be open and honest with you."

"That's what I want too."

"I wouldn't say we are different people than we were back in spring, but I think we both have grown this summer. I think we see life differently than we did previously. Would you agree?"

"I couldn't have said it better."

Laughing, she smiled and said, "Then why are you still on that side of the picnic table?"

Chapter 15

"Bella?"

"Yeah?"

"What happened to your Doc Martens?"

Bella looked down at the shoes on her feet. She looked up at Marge, totally confused. There was nothing different about her Doc Martens. With deep furrows in her brow she asked, "What do you mean?"

"Your Doc Martens, did something happen to them?"

Still totally confused about what Marge was getting at, she dismissively said, "Nooo."

"Well, something must have happened. They appear to be much lighter as there is a spring in your step and a grace to your stride that I have not witnessed all summer."

"Ha-ha. Very funny, Marge." The weight of the sarcasm could easily have crushed a sumo wrestler.

Bella moved to the other side of the store to avoid any further conversation with Marge. It wasn't so much that she minded the conversation with Marge. It was the ears of her colleagues that grew in size that bothered her. It was not any of their business why she had a spring in her walk. Plus, she needed a moment to ponder how it was that Marge knew something was different. Marge always knew how she was feeling, what she needed to hear, and… and… the shoes. What was it with Marge and the shoes?

Chapter 16

Over the next week, there had not been a single evening that had not placed Brent in the presence of Bella.

The two-a-day football practices were a killer, but Brent managed to stay awake long enough to get through supper and watch the opening of a TV show before falling asleep with his head in Bella's lap. Bella didn't mind that he fell asleep. It allowed her to turn off the TV and read while Brent snored away.

Bella's mom also welcomed the change to the evening dynamics. Having Brent in the house was an easy transition. He was not only respectful but helpful. If she needed muscle to complete a household chore, Brent was always willing to help. She also enjoyed seeing more of Bella rather than having her secluded in her bedroom.

Bella had never shared the full story of what happened the night of prom or the details surrounding why she and Brent stopped dating. Her mom asked several times but realized Bella wasn't going to share. Her mom concluded the reason for the breakup wasn't too serious since they were back together.

The evening before the season's first football game, Brent informed Bella that the coach had implemented a new team policy. The night before a game, the players would eat supper together at a parent's house. That meant he would not be able to eat supper with her, but he promised he would come over afterwards.

Smiling, Bella told him that it actually worked out well because she had to close that evening in order to be able to attend the game on

Friday night.

*　*　*

Thursdays at Rerun Thrift Store were generally one of slower days. Bella discovered, after a month of employment and having worked each day of the week, that each day had its own unique characteristics. Mondays tended to be a day, like Saturdays, when receiving drop-offs was a significant part of the workload. It was also the day when midday bathroom cleaning took place. According to Marge, both factors were a result of the store being closed on Sunday. Tuesday was the day to make sure that all items were in the proper place throughout the store. Items had a mysterious way of moving from one section to another. Matching pairs of gloves would be separated, one glove found among baby items and the other in furniture. Women's blouses would be tucked in among men's shirts. And of course, *L* was found with *M*, and *XXL* among *S*. Wednesdays were all-hands-on-deck. The store would be crowded with locals in need of essentials and others from across town looking for good deals. Thursday was the day to pick up from Wednesday, to bring forth new items to the floor and do a deep cleaning in preparation for the weekend. Fridays and Saturdays were the two days that ran full staffing from the moment the doors opened until they were locked.

It was a bit of a surprise when Marge informed Bella that the local retirement center would be dropping off several boxes of items late Thursday afternoon.

"Before you leave tonight, would you rummage through the boxes with shoes and toss those that are damaged or beyond salvaging?"

"You want me to dig through the boxes from the old folks home?"

"Yes, and it's the retirement center. Is that a problem?"

"Old folks home, rest home, convalescent home, nursing home, it doesn't matter what you call it, a pig with lipstick is still a pig."

"Bella?"

"Oh, come on, Marge. You know the smell that fills the storage room the moment those boxes are opened. And the shoes are the worst."

"You are exaggerating. But… that's why we need to go through the boxes. Some of the shoes will be too worn to be placed on the wall. I don't want the boxes sitting here all weekend. The shoes that are not resalable, place them in the dumpster."

"I have a quick and easy solution. How about we place the entire box unopened in the dumpster."

"How about you do what you are hired to do? Enough said?" It wasn't very often that Marge spoke to Bella in such a manner, but when she did, it was clear, she was the boss.

"Yeah, I suppose." Bella ran her hands through her hair. This wasn't what she expected for a Thursday.

* * *

The cardboard boxes could not contain the odor that was embedded in each item packed within. Bella's nose burned the moment she stepped into the storage room. It was worse than the bathroom she just left. The odor was an odd mixture of pee, disinfectant, body sweat, overly sweet grandma perfume, Brut aftershave lotion, Vicks, and just a hint of poop.

Bella decided that if the old folks home was going to send over monthly boxes, she would request that Marge order a stink balm odor block or at least some peppermint essential oil.

Pulling on a pair of rubber gloves, she tackled the first box labeled shoes. Most of the pairs still had a piece of masking tape inside the back heel identifying the owner of the shoes. She created two piles, those for the dumpster and those to be sanitized and placed on the north wall. The ratio was nine to one. One pair out of every ten pulled from the box would receive additional attention. Tossing the unwanted shoes back in the first box she opened the second. The contents mirrored the first. It surprised her that old people, who seldom strolled outdoors, who walked from the bed to the bathroom, and three times a day down to the dining room would have such worn, tattered footwear.

Two-thirds of the way through the second box, her hand brushed against something furry and she quickly pulled her arm out for fear it might be a mouse. Slowly she leaned over the edge of the box and peered inside. Feeling silly, she reached for a matted pair of slippers. There was no masking tape identifying the owner, in part because there was not a back to the slippers and because she imagined every worker knew to whom the slippers belonged. There was a small tag on the right slipper stating the lilac-colored footwear was an alpaca slipper with a suede sole.

Even though the fur was matted with strands twisted into knotted clumps, there was still something soft about the slippers. Further inspection revealed that the bottom sole was tissue paper thin in places on both slippers. Her finger with little effort could have penetrated the suede. The little toe area on the left slipper was missing strands of alpaca fur. Without any forethought, she should have tossed the slippers. Yet for some reason, Bella was unable to release the pair from her hands.

She rose from her knees where she had been working and sat on a folding chair. The slippers rested in her lap like an oversized cat lounging. Her curiosity led her to craft stories about who owned such a pair of slippers. Frustrated by the stereotype of the story her mind wrote, she stopped herself. With a smirk, her head tilted forward, and as though the slippers were listening, she said, "My grandma would wear these slippers."

With a slipper in each hand, she left the stinky storeroom and made her way to the dressing room. If everything worked as she expected, before long she would see the person to whom the slippers once belonged.

"My name is Sofie."

Bella heard the voice, but the image in the mirror had not spoken. Her lips never moved. From where was the voice coming? Bella's question was interrupted before her mind could resolve the dilemma.

"Sofie means wisdom. I have much to share if you are willing to listen?"

Softly, as though speaking in the presence of a sleeping baby, Bella asked, "Are you speaking to me?"

"Of course, my dear, to whom else would I be speaking? It is, after all, just you and me, and... those you are about to meet."

"Others? I... I don't see others. I don't even see you speaking. Your lips don't move. The image I see in the mirror... Are you the one..."

"Am I the one speaking? I have much to share with you, but only if you are willing to listen. Sit back and listen. Close your eyes if you must. To hear is more important than to see. Anyone can believe who sees, but it demands true faith to only hear and still believe."

As had become her custom, Bella scooted back until she touched the wall. She closed her eyes and waited to hear what she could not see. The voice she waited to hear cracked and shook. It was strong with passion yet weak in volume. Bella would need to twist her head from side to side to enable her ear to collect the words from the old, barefoot woman standing clothed in a long cotton floral print nightie.

"I don't live in the world. I live in another realm. Sadly, a world others can't see as they are blinded by their own world. I see, I smell,

I touch, I taste, I hear things others do not. Oh, I fought against it. I shouted. I shook my fist. I hit those closest to me. I even struck myself, to make me feel what the world feels, but it did not stop me from leaving one world to enter another."

"You want to know the most painful part of this move? For a time, a time that was too long, I had a foot in each world. For a time, when I looked into the eyes of family and friends of the world, the world I was leaving, I saw pity. And so, I thought this must be bad. I concluded this was hell. Everything I valued, everything I was taught and told and accepted as truth, as important, was disappearing from my mind. I must be crazy, or the eyes of others would not be darkened with worry."

The voice ceased.

Bella opened her eyes to see if the image was still standing. The old woman had not moved. Bella closed her eyes again and waited. She trusted the voice would return.

"The world into which I stepped was so clear. It was the world of my past. But sadly, it was a world family and friends refused to see. When I spoke of this world, they smiled, but I saw the shallowness of their expressions. They were scared. Those not scared, who didn't shy away, were the young, the very young. It was as though they saw and heard my world. They understood how I could talk to stuffed animals and the animals would respond with grace. The young, the very young, along with the animals of your world, dogs and cats and horses understood. We communicated with a voice deep inside. We spoke from the soul.

"Let me ask you, young lady, how is it that you hear me in my world? How is it you don't demand I meet you in your world? How is it that you have stepped into my world? I look at you, and I don't see pity or sadness within you. I see only openness and a curiosity to meet me. How is that?"

Embarrassed, Bella whispered a reply, "I am wearing your slippers?"

"My slippers?" The voice grew strong. "What slippers?"

Bella opened her eyes and lifted her leg to the figure locked in the mirror.

Sofie shouted, "My alpaca slippers, you stole my slippers!"

"No, Sofie, your slippers were delivered to the store." "Store? My child, you do not make sense."

"I don't know this for sure," Bella said, "but I assume the old folks home took your

slippers because they are worn out."

"I don't know of that which you speak, my dear child. I only say that because I have no slippers. I am pushed about in an oversized baby stroller."

Gripping the bottom of the left slipper, Bella asked, "Do you wish for me to return the slippers to you?"

"Come, come into my world, a world in which there is no need for slippers. Let me show you my family and friends who love me as I am. Close your eyes and come. Walk with me in my world."

For the longest period, Bella sat engulfed in silence. She saw nothing with her mind's eye. She was afraid that she, like all the other people of the world, could not see the world in which Sofie lived the final days of her earthly life. Growing restless and impatient with herself, she stole a peek at the mirror with a partially opened left eye. "Crap!" was all she uttered as both eyes opened wide.

The figure in the mirror had vanished. Sofie was gone. She had returned to her world, a world that Bella concluded she could not enter. With her legs pulled up against her body, she rested her chin on her knees and felt miserable. She felt sorry for Sofie that she was unable to visit her world. She felt sorry for herself. It was a feeling she absolutely despised. With a simple shake of her head that tossed her hair from side to side, she decided rather than continue to feel sorry for herself, she would replay the words Sofie had spoken.

"Come, come into my world, a world in which there is no need for slippers. Let me show…" Bella stopped abruptly. She repeated aloud a portion of the words. "A world in which there is no need for slippers." No need for slippers. Was it possible? Could she continue to communicate with Sofie without wearing the slippers? Were the slippers holding her back? Did she trust the slippers more than Sofie, more than herself?

She straightened out her legs and observed the tattered and worn alpaca slippers. From a distance, the slippers resembled roadkill, a furry ball of nothing. With more difficulty than she anticipated, Bella lifted her right leg a couple of inches from the floor, hooked the toe of the left slipper to the back of the right, and pressed forward. The slipper flew from her foot, reaching a height of three, maybe four feet. She repeated the action with the left and the toes of her right foot.

A strange sense of nakedness crept upon her. It was just slippers she told herself, but she knew it was more than slippers. Slippers that rested against the mirror. A mirror that only held her reflection. A shrug of her shoulders was an attempt to convince herself that she had nothing to lose. Sofie was no longer present with the slippers on her feet, why not… why not trust…

With her legs again pulled tight against her body, she closed her eyes and waited.

The wait was not long. The silence was interrupted by Sofie's faint, raspy voice.

"This is Teddy. Teddy likes it when I rub his nose. Do you want to rub his nose?"

Bella heard but she did not see. The world from which Sofie spoke was not visible. She thought about informing Sofie that Teddy was not visible but stopped herself for fear she might lose the ability to hear.

"What's the matter, dear child? Do you not like Teddy?"

Bella's immediate thought was to lie, to play along, but this was not a game for Sofie. She was all too aware that lying was part of the world Sofie had left. What she didn't know was if it was part of Sofie's new world. She finally concluded that lying was not an acceptable option. Bella spoke, "I am sorry, Sofie, but I don't see Teddy. I don't see you."

"Of course, you can't see Teddy. Turn around. You are staring at a blank wall. A wall I call the wall of nothingness."

The sense of foolishness evaporated as quickly as she twirled about. Sofie was holding a brown furry Teddy bear.

Chapter 17

"The wall of nothingness. You do know it's not really a wall. It's just nothingness. I call it a wall because it seems to create a boundary, a border of sorts. It's safe and yet dangerous. It's enticing, yet deadly. It doesn't make any demands, yet it also doesn't offer anything in return. It's just nothingness."

Bella turned her head and scanned the nothingness as Sofie continued.

"Having said all that, it must be stated that the wall of nothingness can become a place where one is lost forever. The nothingness has no beginning and no ending. It just *is*. it is void of all meaning and purpose."

Bella directed her eyes back to Sofie and then slowly shook her head. Her words followed, "I never was much of a philosopher. I…" She paused for several seconds. "I don't get it. I don't understand how nothingness can exist if it is nothing." When she ended her response, her shoulders were touching her earlobes.

Sofie never hesitated. She answered immediately. "The mind goes blank. It ceases to be. Therefore, escape, return from the wall, from nothingness, occurs only if another entity calls to you. If another invites you to return, to activate your mind."

She waited as Bella pondered the notion of a mind being blank and being activated. She waited and watched for the moment when Bella's eyes made contact with her eyes. The moment they connected, Sofie pushed on.

"For a period of time, when I still had a foot in both worlds, I thought that nothingness was all that awaited me in this world. I didn't see or hear anything. Each time my body leaned into the world my mind went blank. I sounded foolish because the people in your world only heard incomplete sentences. They encountered the silence of my inability to respond. But the more I left your world, the more I discovered that I was staring at the wall of nothingness. I discovered that there was a whole other world awaiting my arrival."

"You make it sound so... so good. You make it sound as though this world is better than the world you left. The world I know."

"Good? Better? Maybe we should simply call it *different*."

"Different might be an understatement. There is no such thing as a wall of nothingness in the world you once lived in, and I still do."

"My dear child, you are beginning to see. You are so correct. The fear was so great within my soul. I feared for a time that I might become nothing. But as I learned, as I moved further away from one world and into another, I discovered there is more to this world. As you can see with Teddy." Sofie smiled wide as she asked, "You do feel his presence, yes?"

"I do. I mean... I think I do." Bella struggled to define what she felt.

"Enough talk. Come. Come and see and hear my world."

Bella didn't move.

Sofie saw Bella's apprehension and its source. She carefully delivered the words to calm her fears.

"The purpose, dear child, of this journey is not to prepare you for something in your future. Not everyone enters this world. You may never enter here as a permanent resident. Of that, I do not know. The purpose is for you to understand that you need not pity those of us who do enter this world."

Bella's sigh of relief was cut short by a voice calling for Sofie.

"Come," Sofie said to Bella. "Come and see my mama."

"Your mama?" Bella thought *how is that possible? I don't know the age of Sofie, but I can't believe her mama is still alive.* "Your mama is still living?" The words slipped out.

"Yes, but not as you think of living. Living as I see them."

The woman who called out to Sofie was much younger than Sofie. Her hair was brunette, the skin on her face was tight. She wore a long dress with an apron. Her cheeks were white, but not with makeup but with… flour. The smell of freshly baked cookies was captivating.

"Sofie, come quickly if you wish to help bake the cookies." The aroma of peanut butter cookies made Bella lick her lips. She could taste the cookies. The soft warm dough melted in her mouth.

Sofie, speaking to Mama as a child of six or seven, announced how these were her favorite cookies, even better than chocolate chip cookies.

The scene jumped, and Sofie pulled Bella with her as they journeyed deeper into the world.

A man, a handsome, well-groomed man, bounced a child, hardly more than three years of age, on his foot as though the child was riding a horse. The child giggled and screamed with joy. The man, who the child called Daddy, laughed and kicked his leg even higher into the air. Daddy was even younger than the woman called Mama. Sofie too was younger. Bella felt the movement, up and down, up and down, and realized the world enabled Sofie to remember an event blocked in the world she left. Here, Sofie could recall events and see people that were no longer visible in the world to which Bella would return.

Papa, an old man with white whiskers to match his white thinning hair, squeezed an accordion. Inward he pushed and outward pulled the instrument as he sang and yodeled *Mei Vater ist ein Appenzeller.*

His granddaughter Sofie, five years-old, twirled about in perfect time to the music. Each word was sung in German, and Sofie sang along. Even Bella, who did not speak a single word of German knew of what they sang. As the tempo increased and Papa pushed and pulled and his finger flew over the keys and buttons of the accordion, Sofie spun faster and faster and faster until her twirling was a blur of grace.

Bella sat next to a Christmas tree. Sap from the blue spruce dripped onto her shoulder. Beneath the tree, lit with multiple colored glass bulbs, were a handful of presents, six in total. Three for each person who sipped a glass of wine and shared the space on a loveseat. The last present opened belonged to Sofie. It was a gift from her husband Alfred. The paper, unlike the other gifts, was not Christmas paper but bright red tissue paper. Sofie, a middle-aged woman, carefully removed the paper so as not to tear it. Inside the box was a pair of slippers. Alpaca slippers, lilac in color. As she leaned over to kiss Alfred, the picture changed. It was another Christmas, but only one gift was beneath a tree. The box was wrapped in bright red tissue paper. Sofie, as she had done the previous year, carefully unwrapped the gift. Inside was the same pair of Alpaca slippers. She leaned over, but there was no one to kiss. Her husband passed away weeks after Christmas the previous year.

Fifteen more times, Bella sat next to a Christmas tree. Each time there was only one gift. A box wrapped in bright red tissue paper and inside was the same pair of slippers, only more worn with each opening.

Bella encountered dogs that chased Sofie across the backyard and dogs that she hugged in moments of needing comfort. There were stuffed animals in all shapes and sizes that came to life as Sofie ran her fingers over and through the furry hide. There were schoolmates and adults in all shapes and sizes from long ago who came to life as Sofie spoke their names and reenacted an encounter.

Taking leave of Sofie, stepping back into her world, back into the dressing room, Bella opened her eyes and looked at herself in the mirror. She stared at herself for a long time trying to understand all that she had seen and heard. She did not possess any evidence, any quantitative data to prove what she just experienced was true, yet she knew it was. She had just been invited into Sofie's mind. The world she had entered was the world of Sofie's mind. The wall of nothingness were those sections of her brain that could no longer be penetrated or no longer existed. The pictures, the scenes, the voices, and the images were all things from Sofie's life that she was experiencing again and again and again.

The slippers that lay at the base of the mirror were added to Bella's reflection as she held them in her hands. Carefully, she slid her hands into each slipper and felt the worn suede sole. A soul so vulnerable to penetration. As she whispered, she watched her lips move. It was the first time she ever focused on herself as she spoke.

"Thank you, Sofie. Thank you for inviting me to experience, to feel, the warmth of your soul."

Chapter 18

"I want to go bowling."

"You what? I don't think I heard you correctly." The front tire of the car struck the curb and climbed onto the boulevard. Brent couldn't believe what he just heard. Fortunately, they had just arrived at Bella's home and the car wasn't traveling more than five miles an hour.

"You heard me. I want to go bowling tomorrow night."

"I may have heard you, but I certainly don't understand."

"What's to understand?"

Putting the car in reverse, Brent backed the front tire off the boulevard and onto the street. With the car in park, Brent turned to look at Bella as he explained. "I remember, shortly after we started going out last spring, you explained why you didn't go out with me when I asked you to go bowling. You said, and I quote, 'I don't wear other people's shoes.'"

"Yeah, well, maybe it's time I try."

Brent shook his head and said, "I don't think you are being honest with me. There is something else going on here."

"Look, either you want to go bowling or you don't." Bella reached for the door handle.

Brent reached across the front seat and grabbed Bella's other arm. "Wait. Of course, I want to go bowling. I'm just trying to understand why you want to go."

Bella turned back and said, "Isn't it enough that I want to go?" She then leaned closer and kissed him. "What time should we go?"

With Bella not pulling back, Brent was nearly speaking into her mouth. "Saturday evenings are usually a busy time. I would suggest we either go early or wait and go later. From about six until nine, it's generally families with younger kids."

Bella pulled back further and was smiling. "I have an idea. Let's go out for pizza and then get to the bowling alley sometime after nine. My treat."

"You're paying, your decision. Do you work tomorrow?"

"Only a couple of hours. With Halloween only a month away, the store is really busy on Saturdays. Marge would like everyone available to work. I should be able to leave by six."

* * *

"Strike! You're a hustler, aren't you?" Brent could not believe it. Bella's first ball, despite rolling slower than molasses ... knocked down all ten pins.

Laughing and jumping up and down, Bella said, "I think they call that beginner's luck."

"We'll see. You got nine more frames." Brent was still baffled.

Waiting for Brent to return, having bowled his first ball and creating a 7/10 split, Bella said, "How about we place a little bet on this game?"

Cooling his fingers over the fan, Brent turned and said, "See, I told you, you're a hustler."

"No, I just feel confident that I can win." Bella couldn't control her smile. She was teasing him, and she loved it.

Taking a seat next to Bella, Brent calmly said, "Okay, what's the bet?"

"If I win, we will do whatever I want tomorrow, no questions asked. If you win, you determine what we do tomorrow, no questions asked.

Agreed?"

The crease in his brow deepened. With a slight tilt of his head, he asked, "What's this all about, Bella? You have something up your sleeve."

She reached out and took his hand in hers. "If I do, there's only one way to find out."

After a moment of nodding his head several times, he smiled, and said, "Yeah, sure, why not. I'll bet. I like my odds."

She turned and looked at the 7/10 split and said, "So, do I. So… do… I!"

* * *

"So, what's the plan for tomorrow, Bella?"

"You'll find out tomorrow when you pick me up at one o'clock."

Holding the door open as they exited the bowling alley, Brent continued to ask for clarity. "What should I wear? Do I need a full tank of gas?"

Without stopping or turning to face him directly, Bella answered, "The way you are dressed now is just fine. As for gas, we can always buy more if needed."

"You're not going to give me any clues, are you? You are enjoying this way too much!" Although Brent was playful, he also was serious. It annoyed him, first that he lost, and then second, that Bella would not provide any details.

Siding into the passenger's seat, she said, "A bet is a bet. No questioning."

* * *

Brent arrived one minute before one o'clock. Before he reached the front door, Bella emerged carrying a small box wrapped in bright red tissue paper.

"Gift for me?"

"You wish. Nope, it's for the person we are going to visit."

Watching her pass by him and heading for the car, Brent called out, "Care to tell me the person's name?"

"Not really. But it wouldn't help you anyway. You have never met this person."

Siding into the driver seat with his hand on the key, he paused, looked at Bella, and asked, "So, no name, an address?"

Looking straight ahead, she smiled and replied. "I don't know the address."

"Great. So how are we supposed to find this person? Or will they find us?"

"Oh, stop being such a sore loser. I know how to get there. I just don't know the address."

"Sore loser? I…"

She cut him off. "Yeah, you heard me, sore loser." She then looked at him, reached over, and rubbed his shoulder. "That's why I love you. Now let's get going. I'll tell you when to turn."

The engine roared to life, and the word *love* roared in his head and heart.

* * *

Pulling into the parking lot, Brent said, "Hey, this is the Loving, Caring Nursing Home. You know someone here? Wait, is your grandma here now?"

"Grandma? Oh, God no." The suggestion of grandma in an old folks home made her laugh. She wouldn't survive. They would kick her out for being too ornery and cantankerous. "No, I met someone recently, and she resides here."

Stepping into Sofie's room, they saw her slouched over in her wheelchair. She looked as though she might be dead.

Brent lowered his head and whispered to Bella, "It smells in here."

"You have never been in an old folks home, have you?"

"No."

"You get used to it after a while."

"That's not really comforting."

Bella decided it was best to change the subject. "You know what she called her wheelchair? A large baby stroller. It's that clever?"

"So, how do you know her?"

Bella ignored the question and moved closer to Sofie. She softly placed her hand on Sofie's shoulder and called out. "Sofie, Sofie, it's Bella. I brought you something I want you to have."

Slowly, Sofie was roused from her sleep, opened her eyes, and tilted her head back to see from where the noise came.

"Hi, Sofie. It's Bella. I have a gift for you." She showed Sofie the small box wrapped in bright red tissue paper. You want to open it, or should I unwrap it for you?"

Sofie never moved. Her eyes blinked and a bit of drool dropped from the corner of her mouth.

"Find me a Kleenex," she said to Brent.

Bella wiped Sofie's mouth and chin. "How about you watch me open the gift? I promise I will be careful not to tear the paper."

With the tissue paper set to the side and the cover off, Bella lifted a worn and tattered pair of alpaca slippers from the box and showed them to Sofie.

She lifted her head an inch, maybe two, to gain a better view of the slippers.

Bella brought the slippers close to Sofie's cheek, and said, "Feel how soft they still are. I will put them on your feet." She knelt down and carefully lifted Sofie's frail legs, one at a time, and slid the alpaca slippers on. "There, just like the very first time."

Brent was totally confused by what he was witnessing. Bella spoke to this old woman as though she had known her all her life. How could that be? Bella said they met recently. He was too overwhelmed to speak.

"Sofie, have you been horseback riding recently? It's a beautiful day for a ride."

Sofie didn't respond. She did not acknowledge that she heard all the tales that Bella spoke, but it didn't stop Bella from talking.

"Sofie, before we go, I have one more surprise I wish to share with you." Bella pulled her phone from her pocket. She tapped on the face of the phone. "This is not Papa. It's a group called Alpensterne." Music filled the room. The words *Mei Vater ist ein Appenzeller* echoed about the four walls.

Bella reached for Brent's hand and together they swayed back and forth in rhythm to the music. As the song ended, Bella leaned in close to Sofie and said, "I hope you enjoyed the dance. You looked so graceful."

A knock at the door brought a nurse into the room. "Good afternoon, Sofie. Oh, I see you have guests. Welcome. Sofie, I have your afternoon medicine and your favorite cookie. A chocolate chip cookie."

Bella didn't hesitate to correct the nurse. "Her favorite is peanut butter."

"Sorry?" The nurse turned, clearly confused, and looked at Bella.

"Her favorite cookie is peanut butter, not chocolate chip."

The nurse straightened up and towered over Bella who remained seated. "I'm sorry, the staff told me she likes chocolate chip."

Bella looked at Sofie as she responded, "Yeah, she likes chocolate chip, but her favorite is peanut butter. When she was a little girl, she used to help her mother bake peanut butter cookies."

The nurse never questioned Bella, she simply said, "Good to know. I will remember that and try to bring her peanut butter cookies."

Stepping back from Sofie, confident the pill had been swallowed, the nurse nearly shouted, "Sofie, where did those slippers come from? I thought we had thrown them away?"

She looked at both Brent and Bella for answers.

Bella merely shrugged her shoulders and added, "She was wearing them when we came into the room." She remembered how easy it was to lie in this world.

The nurse stated, "They are so beaten up and I'm just afraid she will fall wearing them."

Softly Bella asked, "Does she walk?"

"Well, no, not really, but…" After a pregnant breath, she continued, "I suppose it's okay that she wears them when she is in the wheelchair."

Brent wanted so much to say *large baby stroller*, but he bit his lip.

Bella couldn't be sure, but it looked as though the corners of Sofie's lips turned upward just slightly.

As Bella reached the door, ready to leave, she turned back and said, "Sofie, say hi to Teddy for me."

Chapter 19

The moment they stepped outside of the Loving, Caring Nursing Home, Brent inhaled deeply. "Fresh air." After several additional deep, cleansing breaths, Brent looked directly into Bella's eyes and said, "What was that all about?"

She stepped forth, kissed him softly, and then said, "I promise I will tell, but first I want you to take us to the lake. I will tell you everything on the shore."

Brent stood dumbfounded. He spoke very slowly, "Are you sure, the lake?"

"Yes." The word was delivered with confidence.

"First, bowling, and now the lake. Bella, I can't keep up with you."

She smiled flirtatiously as she said, "That's a good thing, right?"

As they neared the lake, Bella directed Brent to park in the same location as he had the night of prom.

With a blanket from the trunk, the couple walked hand in hand along the edge of the lake until they spotted a clearing where the sand was not covered with weeds from the lake. The afternoon sun warmed the sand while the breeze blew across their backs and kept the fishy smell of fall at bay.

They sat in silence and watched a tiny boat across the lake bob up and down. Brent vowed to himself that he would be patient and not press Bella to speak until she was ready. Bella rehearsed over and over how best to start. Concluding there was no best way she opened her mouth and trusted the right words would flow forth.

"Before I start, I need you to not interrupt me until I finish. I promise I will try to answer any questions, but once I start, I need to finish. Agreed?

"Yes, of course." Brent nodded to make sure Bella knew he fully agreed.

"I asked to come here because I want you to know that I completely trust you. For the longest time, the lake represented my inability to trust, to trust you and anyone who tried to get close to me. But when it comes to you, that is no longer true. Brent, I trust you one hundred percent." She raised her hand, sensing he was about to speak.

He nodded his head. He was about to interrupt her to let her know that he also trusted her.

"What I am about to share with you, I can't fully explain. It's beyond comprehension, but I know it's true. Or at least, I believe it's true." She stopped, closed her eyes, and inhaled. She held the air within… held it in… held it in… and finally exhaled. She opened her eyes, reached for his hands, and then continued.

"It all started last year, late one evening when I was closing up the Rerun Thrift Store. I had just finished cleaning the bathroom. I was preparing to leave the building when my eye caught a pair of wine-colored stilettos with an ankle strap and a four-and-a-half-inch heel. It was as though the shoes were crying out *try me on*. To understand the degree of temptation you need to know that I love shoes. Even though the thought of trying on someone else's shoes was disgusting, I just had to see what those shoes looked like on me. But here's the thing: they were a size eleven, yet the moment my foot slid in, the shoe magically—I don't know any other way to describe it—the shoes magically formed to my feet. My entire body started to tingle. Something unexplainable was happening. I stepped into the dressing room to see what the shoes looked like on me, but I didn't see my reflection. Instead, I saw the owner, the woman to whom the shoes once belonged."

She stopped and looked at Brent for any sign of disbelief. Listening to herself recount the story, she found it difficult to accept. It sounded like some cheap sci-fi movie aired on a cable network no one watched.

Brent just smiled and waited for her to continue. He squeezed her hands encouraging her.

She went on to describe each pair of shoes she tried on and the characters she met. She emphasized how each encounter was slightly different and how at first that was alarming, but now she came to understand that it forced her to keep an open mind to what was transpiring. Reluctantly, she spoke of Marge and a growing suspicion that somehow, she was a part of the whole experience.

"I can't explain it," Bella said, "but it's as though Marge stimulates a part of my thinking and then I find a pair of shoes that, well, aligns with what Marge was just discussing. It could all be just a coincidence, but something in my gut says there is more to it."

At first, unraveling the events of the past year, Bella did not mention how she purchased the flip-flops and then other pairs of shoes. But as the details rolled forth, she decided she had to tell him everything.

"I… oh, this is so embarrassing. I bought the flip-flops." She described how employees were not allowed to buy items from the store, but how Marge made a one-time exception. She followed that critical piece of information with the following confession.

"I also bought a pair of baby shoes that I gave back to the mother and Sofie's slippers. Well, I didn't actually buy them. I saved them from landing in the garbage bin."

As though exhausted from talking for the better part of an hour, Bella sat still. She wasn't exhausted, she was merely making sure she had not neglected to share any important details. Trusting that Brent would seek clarity if a detail or two was missing, she offered a warm smile. She pressed her body forward, and said, "I guess that's it. Questions?"

"Wow." It was clear Brent was still trying to take it all in. He shook his head a couple of times as though trying to clear a path to proceed. When he finally spoke, his words were delivered with sincerity and earnestness, but also with confidence.

"This may not be the first question you expected me to ask, but it's what I've been thinking about since you started. Last night, when we were bowling, did you see or feel the owner of the bowling shoes?"

Bella let go of his hands and leaned back. She stared at him for several seconds. Her demeanor changed. There was rigidity and hardness that previously did not exist. Her body stiffened, her jaw tightened. It felt as though Brent was probing her abilities. It was one thing for her to share her experiences. She was in control of that conversation. It was an entirely different conversation to answer such a question. She elected to respond cautiously. "You're right. You are absolutely right. That's not the question I anticipated."

She turned and looked out across the lake to see if the tiny boat was still bobbing. Much to her dismay, it was gone. She wasn't sure why that was disheartening. Maybe it was that she needed an anchor at the moment to keep her from lashing out or fleeing. She scanned the horizon and concluded that even the sun, which drifted behind the trees, had abandoned her. Soon it would be dark, the night air would be crisp, and it would bite against her cheeks. She lifted her hand to stroke her cheek and discovered she already felt the chill, but not necessarily from the falling temperature. She invited him to ask questions. He was only following her directive. She needed to set aside the shock that ripped through her body and respond.

She cleared her throat and with a voice that wavered, she said, "No. I did not see or feel the owner of the shoes. Bowling shoes are not owned. They are rented. Plus, and I guess I didn't make this clear, I'm not quite sure what role the mirror in the dressing room plays, or the store for that matter. I think it has something to do with it. Something special is happening there."

Realizing the change in Bella, Brent asked, "Are you upset with me?"

She pulled her legs up tight against her body before she answered. "Upset? No." She gave herself time to select the word that best described what she felt. "Confused, would be a better word."

Before seeking clarity, he reached out and touched her forearm. "What's confusing?"

She ignored the weight of his hand and whispered, "I don't know." She paused before saying more. "It's going to sound childish."

"You said you trusted me... now you're telling me I would call you childish? Bella, if you trust me, then you know I would never call you childish. What's confusing?"

She relaxed slightly and that was just enough for the tear ducts to open. With her fingertips, she swept away the droplets and said, "That's the problem. Everything is confusing. I'm confused by your response, I'm confused what's happening to me, I'm confused what it all might mean, assuming it really is happening."

Without saying a word, Brent moved next to her, wrapped his arms around her, and pulled her next to his body. He held her. He held her as he had done the night of prom, but not to satisfy himself, but because he realized he loved her. He held her because she needed to be held.

As she stirred, he loosened his hold and waited for her to respond. She lifted her head and their eyes met. As the water peacefully rolled up onto the sandy beach, their lips found each other. At that moment, words were not needed to convey the message. They were giving themselves over to the other. They were entrusting the moment and the future in the hands of the other. Neither uttered the words *I love you* but each felt the love that the other had to share. There would be plenty of time for speaking the words. Right now, it was enough to just feel it.

At the risk of polluting the moment, Brent decided to push back the silence. He asked, "What do you need from me?"

Bella ran her fingers through her hair to remove several strands that hung across her face. She shook her head to ensure the hair stayed back, and then she spoke. "I need you to help me understand what is happening. I need you to support me with what is happening to me and maybe even through me."

"Through you, you think…"

Without letting him finish, Bella interrupted, "Yeah, maybe. I don't know. I have wondered, am I being used for something? There has to be a reason for all of this, right? I mean, things like this just don't happen without a reason, right?"

Brent turned his body so he could face her directly and asked. "And you think this might be where Marge comes in?"

"That's just it, I don't know. I don't know." She brought her hand to her forehead and let it drop over her entire face. "I think so one moment, but then." The weight of what she was suggesting silenced her for a moment. "Days, weeks, go by, and nothing. And when it does happen, it's all so, so subtle. It is only after the fact that I wonder, is she part of all this? If so, how? Why?"

He sensed she was again being consumed by uncertainty. To stop her from fading like the sun that was sinking, he asked, "Bella, what do you want from me right now, what can I do?"

Her eyes met his and she said, "Hold me. Tell me I am not crazy."

With a smile and a slight shake of his head, he said, "You are not crazy." To lighten the moment, he added, "Beautiful, yes. Crazy, no."

She smiled to match his and pressed on. "I… I want you to come to the store and see for yourself what happens to me. I want to know if you too see and hear what I do. Or if it's all in my head. Am I… am I schizo?"

"Tell me when, and I'll be there." And he reached out and pulled her next to his body and held her.

Chapter 20

The Saturday before Halloween, as expected, was chaos.

The store hosted an endless stream of visitors. The last-minute costume hunters were the worst. They fit into one of two categories. They either had such an elaborate vision for their costume and were unable to find the necessary accessories, or they had no plan and were hoping for inspiration to strike as they wandered through the store. No one wanted to assist either of these types of shoppers because it was next to impossible to satisfy them. Individuals from the first group shouted at the employees because the store did not carry the items they needed, while individuals from the second group shouted because the employees were not solving their dilemma of what to wear for Halloween.

Bella marveled that in the weeks before Halloween and Christmas, customers forgot that the merchandise available at the Rerun Thrift Store depended upon what goods were donated. Other than a few toiletries that Marge purchased to sell, everything else was donated.

Having just finished listening to a customer complain that the store didn't have a single item on her shopping list, Bella was proud of herself on two levels. Level one, she successfully assisted the customer in broadening the possibilities of their costume to include a scarf, which completed their ensemble. Level two, not once, during the entire exchange, did she remind the customer that this was a thrift store.

Exhausted and in need of a break, she made her way to the front door. She hoped a few minutes of fresh air would get her through the rest of the day. As her hand landed on the door handle, she heard her name.

"Bella? Bella, do you have a minute?"

She didn't need to turn and see who was calling out her name. She knew Marge's voice. She released the handle and turned to locate Marge.

Marge stood in the doorway of her office next to a table filled with snacks. With her hand, as though she was about to fan herself, Marge waved for Bella to come to the office. As Bella neared, Marge instructed her to grab a snack and come into the office.

Holding a bottle of water in one hand and an apple in the other, Bella dropped into the chair across from Marge. She bit into the apple and felt the droplets of juice escape between her lips and the skin of the apple. It wasn't much of a distraction, but it was something. Before she could sink her teeth into the apple a second time, Marge explained the purpose of her request.

"Earlier this morning we received a shipment of items from a neighboring thrift store. Their storage room is full, and they called asking if we were interested..." Marge raised both hands and stopped herself. Took a deep breath and continued. "None of that matters. As I already said, the shipment arrived this morning. It's quite an assortment of items."

Bella continued to eat her apple as she listened and wondered where this conversation was going and why Marge was telling her all this.

"Because it's been so busy today, we haven't had time to sort through all the items. I was in the back for a while, and..."

Here it comes, Bella thought. She is going to ask me to go work in the back and sort through the items. Bella convinced herself that today such a directive would be just fine.

"And... well, there is a pair of military boots. I am concerned that if we put the boots on the north wall, they could create a problem."

Bella swallowed quickly and said, "A problem? I don't understand."

"The boots could be trouble."

"Trouble? I would think they would be gone in a heartbeat."

"Trouble. Don't you see? The boots could create problems within the store and for anyone who owned them if they lived down by the railroad. The trouble is that the boots will be popular. Every guy," she threw her hands into the air, "maybe every person, is going to want to own those boots. Own them at any cost."

Bella nodded acknowledging that she grasped the problem and potential trouble. She then asked, "Why are you telling me this?"

"Because I want to know what you think we should do with the military boots."

Bella tossed the apple core into the wastebasket, removed the cap from the bottle of water, and drank a fourth of the water. She replaced the cap, looked at Marge, and in a dry tone said, "Don't put them out. Toss them in the garbage bin."

It was now Marge who nodded several times. When she stopped, she said, "Yeah, that's what I thought. I just needed to hear it from someone else. It's a shame though. The boots are in such good condition it seemed like a waste. But… thank you, Bella. You can go get some fresh air and then return to the floor."

The moment she stepped out the front door, her phone was in hand and she was texting Brent.

10:30 tonight at the store. Can U make it? Marge told me about army boots.

Before Bella reached the side of the building and alley, where Marge had placed a picnic table, her phone vibrated with a return message.

Be there! Give details at that time.

* * *

Peering through the window in the door, Brent could see Bella at the opposite end of the store. Half of her body was in the bathroom and the other half was outside. Her headphones obviously kept her from hearing his pounding on the door. He glanced at this watch. 10:15. He knew he was early, but the excitement and anticipation of what awaited him caused his foot to press aggressively on the accelerator.

Afraid that if he continued to pound on the door the noise might result in a phone call to the police, he drove his hands deep into the pockets of his coat. He would just have to wait until ten-thirty or until Bella removed one of the ear cups.

Two minutes before ten-thirty, Bella leaned the mop handle against the wall outside the bathroom, slid the right ear cup of her headphones from her ear, and looked toward the front door. Before Brent's hand was free of his pocket, Bella waved and started across the room.

A quick kiss was followed by Brent saying, "Give me the details, what's up?"

"Good evening to you too."

"Yeah, right, so, where are these army boots?" Brent couldn't control his excitement.

"They're in the back. But slow down. I'll tell you all about it, but first I need to finish mopping the floor in the bathroom. Unless you want to finish mopping and I'll go get the boots."

"I will pass on mopping. I remember the stories you shared about needing to hose down the bathroom. I've waited this long. I can wait another few minutes."

As they sat in the back room with the military boots between them, Bella narrated the story of Marge asking what to do with the boots. When she finished, Brent asked, "Do you believe her, that she needed a second opinion?"

Striking a yoga position, Bella rolled her head in a circle attempting to relieve the tightness in her shoulders and neck that was causing her head to ache. She closed her eyes and inhaled and exhaled twice, sat motionless for a second, and then spoke. "I don't know. It felt so awkward at that moment, but now, without Ronald around to bounce ideas off, she doesn't have anyone." Before she finished the thought, she opened her eyes and looked at Brent for understanding.

Instead, what she received was a shake of the head. Followed by, "It doesn't make sense, Bella. She could have tossed the boots, and no one would have been the wiser. Why bring you into this? It doesn't make sense."

Staring at the army boots, she said, "Yeah, maybe."

Brent too stared at the boots as he probed for clarification from Bella. "What are you going to do? You going to throw them in the garbage bin?"

She looked back and forth between the boots and Brent. "I pulled them from the bin. Marge threw them out sometime before we closed."

"I guess that answers my next question. You plan to put them on?"

"Yeah. I need to find out if there is something special about these boots, beyond the problem Marge suggested."

"And if there is?"

"How about I first put them on and address any issues or problems afterward? Assuming there are problems."

Even though this was totally foreign territory, Brent knew there would be problems. He just couldn't determine or imagine what those might be.

Bella pulled the army boots closer and proceeded to untie the laces that kept the boots as a pair. As the laces dropped and struck the suede coyote-colored leather, she noticed the boots were sprinkled with tiny droplets. Inspecting each boot more closely she was unable to determine if this was part of the original design or if some form of liquid was absorbed and became one with the leather.

Loosening the laces of her shoes, she stopped and said to Brent, "Until this moment, I didn't realize I would be replacing one pair of boots with another pair." A weak smile accompanied the comment.

Brent, now standing, said, "Yeah, but in name only. There is a huge difference between Doc Martens and military-issued boots."

"I suppose. I never really gave it much thought."

"Boots, or the military?"

Extending her hand, waiting for Brent to help her up, she answered, "Oh, God. The military." With a nod of her head to the right, she said, "Let's take these out front and I will put them on there. While I am lacing up, push the sheet to the dressing room back and pull the string for the light."

Brent went ahead and completed the tasks with haste. He didn't want to miss the transformation of the boots to Bella's feet, if there was such a thing. He had tried to sound totally supportive, but he had his doubts. There were just too many details that defied all the laws of nature. As a positivist, he knew he was among those who needed to see to believe.

With her leg in the air and the rubber sole of the army boot coming to rest on Brent's thigh, Bella's words surprised even herself. "I can't believe how light and comfortable this feels on my foot. I think I could stand in these all day. I thought my Docs were comfortable, but…"

Brent interrupted her to remind her she had another boot to put on and then she could stand.

Bella understood her boyfriend's impatience. What he didn't understand was that she could not control the experience that awaited her and that always made her a bit hesitant. Rather than respond, she dropped her foot from his leg, stretched the leather at the top of the other boot, and slid her foot downward.

The precise moment she completed tying a perfect bow, with two evenly matching laces, she stood at attention. She heard a male voice behind her barking out words. Sensing she didn't have permission to turn her head, she cast her eyes to the right and then left. On both sides, less than six inches away, were other individuals. Though she couldn't see their faces, when she lowered her eyes, she saw that they too wore boots just like hers. Staring forward, she blinked several times until she realized that her vision was aided by sunglasses. The scene before her was unfamiliar. Everything was the same color. The color of her boots. It was at that moment that tiny beads of sweat rolled down her sides, and she comprehended how uncomfortable she was. She wasn't just hot. She was overheating. She was sweltering.

Her nausea was interrupted by the voice who barked nonstop. "Okay, gentlemen, you have your orders, load up, and… hey, be safe out there."

"Gentlemen?" the word did not make sense. Who was this person, and why was he referring to her as a man?

"Private, first class? Is there some reason you are not moving?"

She heard herself say, in a voice that did not belong to her, "No sir! Moving, sir!" She was the owner of the boots. As her body climbed into the military armored Humvee, she tried to remember if the officer stated a name? *Who am I?*

The heat inside was just as unbearable as outside. The desert sun penetrated everything.

The conversation among the personnel was casual, yet heavy with the weight of caution. A joke told was followed by playful criticism for sharing such stupidity. A card game was planned for later that evening and the challenge was issued that each of the guys invite a female from the camp with the hope of making the barracks smell better.

The conversation changed as the street narrowed and the driver called out, "Civilians at three o'clock."

A voice behind her, using binoculars, clarified, "Three women."

The inside of the Humvee moved to full alert. "Check the left, check the left."

From her mouth came the words "Watch their hands!" The voice sounded strangely familiar. She needed to hear it more to determine to whom it belonged. But now was not that moment.

"Rooftop, clear." Another voice shouted.

The shotgun passenger intently monitoring the surface of the road, stated, "Path looks undisturbed."

The Humvee passed the three women without incident. A quick exhale by all passengers was interrupted as the soldier seated to the right of the driver, shouted, "Left! Left! Path disturbed to the rig…"

As the Humvee was launched ten feet into the air, it resembled a rocket leaving the launch pad. The vehicle, despite its weight, twirled several times before crashing back down to earth.

The second the tires left the ground Bella's helmet struck the roof of the Humvee with such force that she lost consciousness. Her seatbelt cut into her chest and pinned her against the seat. The soldier to her right ricocheted to every corner when his seat tore loose like a bullet fired in the metal can.

She was stirred to consciousness by the screaming that filled the now half-torn-apart military vehicle. Opening her eyes, she was greeted by blackness. "Focus," she heard the voice within her head saying. "Focus. You have been trained for this. Don't panic." Sickness pushed toward her throat. The voice was familiar.

Using her right arm to gain awareness, she felt the door latch and understood she lay on her left side. With great effort, fighting against the seatbelt that immobilized her body, she directed her arm into the blackness and discovered the blackness was the back of a seat pressed down on her legs. It was only then that she recognized that the screaming was coming from her own body. The pain was beyond anything imaginable. Everything went dark.

She again gained consciousness. The taste in her mouth was acid, and she had thrown up at least once, maybe more. The pain was indescribable. She wiggled her toes, or so she thought. She wasn't sure. And then screamed, "Get me out of these boots." Everything went dark.

She opened her eyes and saw Brent's face only inches from her. Her entire body was crawled against his body, and he was slowly rocking her back and forth. With his hand, he pushed strands of hair from her face and asked, "Are you okay?"

She didn't answer, only inhaled deeply and curled tighter into his body.

When her body finally stopped shaking, Brent asked, "What happened?"

She pulled back slightly and noticed that they were on the floor. Her legs were inside the dressing room and the rest of her body was outside. It sent another shake through her body. She freed herself from Brent and scooted across the floor until she was out of the dressing room. She looked back at Brent and said, "I need some water. There is bottled water in the breakroom."

She sat with her back against the north wall, sipping on the water. Everything came into focus.

Brent, kneeling before her, asked again, "What happened?"

Reaching for his hands, she said, "I will tell you everything, but first I have a question for you."

"A question for me? I don't understand."

"Please, just go with it."

"Okay."

"Brent, have you thought about your future plans? It's not something we have ever really discussed."

"My future plans? You mean like marriage, kids."

"No, more like, what are your plans after graduation."

He took a deep breath and joined her against the wall. He stared out across the room as he attempted to answer her question. "It's sort of up in the air. I am hoping to get a scholarship to play football at a Division One school. I guess if that doesn't happen, I will probably join the army and get the funding I need to go to college."

Remaining composed, Bella asked, "Why the military?"

"I don't know. Service to the country is a huge thing in my family. My grandfather and father served. My brother is in the Secret Service. It's just something one does."

Bella spoke very slowly. Each word was carefully selected. "When I was wearing the army boots, did you look in the mirror?'

Brent wasn't quite sure how to answer. He realized he did have permission to do what he did. "Yeah, I pulled the sheet back slightly and peeked inside, but I didn't see anything."

"You didn't see anyone?"

"No, just my reflection staring back at me."

She knew. Now she knew for sure.

Brent continued, "So tell me. What happened? It was kind of scary. You were rolling about on the floor, and then there was a point when you were screaming, 'Get these boots off me.'"

Bella turned and looked at him, "And you took the boots off?"

"Yeah…" He paused, fearing that maybe he did something wrong. "That was okay, right?"

She smiled, leaned in, and kissed him. "Yeah, that was more than right."

He kissed her a second time and pushed her back slightly. "Are you going to tell me what happened?"

"Yeah, I will tell you, but you have to promise me one thing."

"What's with all these promises?"

She put her finger against his lips and said, "Shh. I need you to promise me that you will never put the army boots on."

He looked totally confused. Shook his head and replied. "Don't worry, my foot would never fit into those boots."

"Are you sure?"

"Of course I'm sure. They're too small."

"I don't think so, dear. I think they would fit you all too well."

"What are you talking about?"

"Brent, this time I didn't journey into the past. I didn't see the owner from afar. I didn't stand beside the owner. I didn't even see the owner of the boots. I became one with the owner of the boots. I experienced everything the owner experienced at that moment."

"You mean, you saw the present?"

"No, I saw the future. I experienced the future as an army personnel. I experienced the future inside the body of the person who would one day own those boots. I was in the desert, someplace in the Middle East. I was in a Humvee that hit a road mine. The owner of those boots, his legs were severed from his body. I felt the pain, Brent. I felt the pain of the owner of those boots. I felt the pain because I know the future owner of those boots."

"I thought you said you didn't see the owner."

"I didn't. But I heard his voice as he spoke. I know his voice. I heard and felt the embarrassment as his buddies teased him about being able to get women to play cards with him because he was a star running back. Brent, I not only saw your future, I experienced it."

"What? You're crazy!" Brent was nearly shouting.

Calmly, tears streaming down her face, she responded. "No, no. I am not crazy. I know what I heard and what I felt. I felt it because

I have given myself to you. Brent, you must promise me that these boots never belong to you. The tiny droplets in the suede are your blood."

"Stop it, Bella! Stop it. This is silly. This is beyond silly. This is sick." Brent stood and raced for the door.

The words that followed him were nearly lost as the door slammed. "Marge, what have you gotten me into?"

Chapter 21

Exactly one week to the day, Brent stood outside the Rerun Thrift Store at 10:15. And just as he had hoped, as he placed both hands against the window and peered inside, he saw Bella half inside and half outside the bathroom. He waited to knock, knowing she would never hear his hand striking the door.

One minute before 10:30, she finished mopping the bathroom and saw his reflection in the window. Opening the door to let him inside, she said, "I didn't expect to see you."

"Me either. But I can't keep avoiding you. We need to talk."

"Not much more to say."

"Did you keep the boots?"

Her head shook. "No. I carried them back to the garbage bin and tossed them inside."

"Thank you."

"You're welcome. I better get back to work. I have a few more things to finish up."

"No, you don't. You always save the bathroom for last, and I saw you finish mopping. You're done." He looked past her and to the bathroom to make sure the light was off. Seeing the darkness, he continued. "Bella, I'm sorry. I shouldn't have stormed out of here. I was scared. I didn't know what to think. I needed time…"

"I understand. But you need to understand that I was just as scared. I'm still scared. I don't understand what this is all about. I don't know what it all means or why me. And…"

"And Marge."

"Yes, and Marge." It made her smile for a second that he knew what she was thinking. "What is her role in all of this?"

"What do you actually know about her?"

"Not much really. I know she has owned this store for several years. She started the business. I know that she is passionate about the poor and homeless. But other than that... nothing."

"Married? Kids?"

"She has never said a word about family. Not to me anyway."

"Maybe my brother can help."

"Can he do that? Will he do that?"

"He's not supposed to, but... I think once I explain, he might be willing to do a little digging."

"Explain? As in, me wearing shoes?"

"Oh, God, no. Just that we have a few questions about her intentions and her business. You know, that sort of stuff."

Bella couldn't pass up the opportunity. She had wanted to inquire about Brent's brother for several weeks but kept putting it off. This was the perfect moment. "Say, if your brother is willing to do that, I have two additional requests. You remember the story about George, the owner of the flip-flops?"

"Yeah."

"I am curious about his daughters and granddaughter. There is something about the granddaughter that keeps gnawing at me."

"And the second request?"

"My dad. Where is he? What happened to him? It's as though he dropped off the face of the earth. My mom will not tell me anything."

"I'm sure he will be willing to follow up on your dad. As for flip-flops, I'll see." Brent closed the space between himself and Bella. "Forgive me?"

"You assume there is something I need to forgive?"

"Yeah, well… you would have good reason to be upset with me."

"I'm not. Like I said, I understand, I am just as confused." She closed her eyes and added, "Kiss me already, you studly star football player."

Chapter 22

The days leading up to Thanksgiving brought additional customers into the store. It was not anything like the Halloween rush or Christmas frenzy, but the store was more crowded. Contributing to the stress of the upcoming holiday, several employees requested additional time off to travel home to be with family. As a result, knowing she would be working all day Friday and Saturday, Bella still volunteered to come in Monday, Tuesday, and Wednesday right after school and stay until closing if needed.

Entering the building on Wednesday afternoon, less than excited to work knowing she would be locked up, Bella told herself that the extra money would be nice.

By six o'clock the crowd was thinning, and Bella was able to relax and catch her breath. The conditions outside were too blustery for a meal at the picnic table, so she retreated to the breakroom. As she entered, she smelled Marge's supper being pulled from the microwave. Marge was a TV dinner junky. Every evening, at least when she was working, she ate a TV dinner. Bella wasn't sure if it was due to enjoying the meals or because they were cheap. She never felt comfortable inquiring why.

The two discussed school, turkey preparations, football, and napping. Bella tried to convince Marge that napping was a part of the first Thanksgiving celebration. They both had a good laugh, all the while totally aware that tomorrow would be just another day.

As Marge disposed of her plastic tray that had conveniently kept the portions of her food separated, Bella asked about a new placement on the north wall.

"When did the ballet shoes come in?"

"Sometime on Monday. They're actually pointe shoes."

"Pointe? What's that?"

"Pointe shoes are the shoes ballet dancers wear to enable them to dance on their toes."

"I thought all ballet shoes did that."

"When you get a chance, check them out. You will notice how they are quite different from what is referred to as a ballet slipper or shoe."

"Well, whatever they are, I can't imagine they will sell very quickly… unless someone wants to use them as a wall hanging."

Marge didn't respond. She smiled, turned, and walked out, leaving Bella alone in the breakroom. It was the first conversation regarding shoes that Marge didn't invest time in. Somehow, that made Bella even more curious about the pointe shoes.

With the front door locked and the bathroom clean, Bella made her way over to the north wall. Lifting the shoes from the shelf, the satin felt so inviting. Pressing her fingers into the shoes, she felt the fabric that had been folded back and forth like ribbon candy, glued, and then compressed to form a platform upon which the toes would stand. She had googled earlier to learn why ballet shoes and pointe shoes were always pink. She had hoped the answer wasn't because pink was for girls.

The answer wasn't much more comforting. To accentuate the leg, dancers wore pale pink tights, to make it appear that the dancer's legs were naked. To keep the eye moving downward, the footwear also had to match the tights. Eventually, like so many things in life, it became a tradition, something no one questioned.

Holding a shoe in each hand, she wondered why she hadn't texted

Brent to come and experience her wearing the shoes. Then she remembered that he was not home. She wondered if she would be able to move into all five ballet positions. She wondered if she would see the owner or become one with the owner. She wondered if… She saw Marge smiling, turning, and leaving her alone in the breakroom. She wondered if Marge had prompted her to take the shoes down from the wall. She wondered…

Music. Music. "Morning Serenade" from Prokofiev's *Romeo and Juliet* swept across the floor of the store. The dressing room was too small to contain the music. It demanded a larger stage upon which to twirl, to swirl, to move about like air itself. It could not be contained; it took control. From the dressing room, Bella floated. The pointe shoes carried her down one aisle and up another. Her feet were above the floor and only now and then did they lightly stroke the surface.

For nearly three minutes she never stopped moving, and then the music stopped. She stood flatfooted, heavy, pressed into the floor. To step was cumbersome. It felt as though the shoes only worked if music played. With the grace of an elephant, she pounded the floor back to the dressing room.

A salty taste invaded her mouth.

"But Mama, I am tired. My legs ache, and my feet hurt. Can't I be done?" The child, curled in a ball with her face hidden between her knees, did not look at the woman with whom she pleaded.

A stern voice connected to a body not visible in the mirror berated the child. "You begged to take ballet. You are not going to quit like you have quit everything else. Now get up and dance." There was a slight hint of an accent but nothing obvious enough for Bella to determine its source.

In between whimpers, a faint response emerged. "I don't want to quit. I just want to be done for today."

In a strange manner, the voice extolled the child's potential talent. "Someday, someday, you will thank me for not permitting you to quit. You are the best student in the class. You could become even better with more practice. I will start the music, and you will practice."

The music started and like a flower unfolding to greet the morning sun. The child unfolded, rose, and began to perform. As the young flower twirled, tiny droplets were sent adrift from her face. Miniature rainbows came and went as rays of sunlight captured the salty droplets. Bella watched and recognized the source of the salt she tasted.

When the music ended, the child dried the tears from her eyes with the back of her hand and used the palms of her hands to wipe her cheeks. Without the presence of a tissue, she sniffed several times to keep her nose from running. She stood in first position and waited for directions. The words came from the same voice.

"You know the routine. Stretch. Twenty minutes of stretching. Take a shower, and then do your homework." Bella had heard the voice three separate times and there was no consistency of when she detected an accent. It was only with certain words. She closed her eyes and attempted to replay each word the woman uttered. It was not an entire word, it was the letter y. It sounded heavy. The young girl's voice broke her focus.

"Yes, Mama."

Next, Bella found herself looking at the top of a table strewn with an array of items that, at first glance, didn't have anything in common. There was cardboard, several rolls of scotch tape and duct tape, a tube of tin foil and a tube of saran wrap, a ball of string, a bottle of glue, a stapler, mini marshmallows, a bar of chocolate, graham crackers, several small pieces of wood, and a packet of papers. It was the packet of papers and the mini marshmallows that alerted Bella to the homework assignment that awaited the young dancer. Every fifth grader in Ms.

Baker's science class had to build a solar oven. The objective was to build an oven to make s'mores.

The scene in the mirror confirmed what Bella guessed about the age of the young girl. She was most likely eleven going on twelve.

The shoes, the same shoes Bella wore, hung from the back of a dining room chair as the young girl struggled to control her frustration. The items on the table did not create anything close to the picture on the last page of the packet. The result was that the packet flew in one direction while the lopsided oven sailed in another.

The adult voice, still not visible, spoke, "You will clean up that mess and start over."

"But Mama. I could really use your help. I don't understand the directions."

"Building the oven for you will not help you."

"I'm not asking you to do it for me, just to help me understand how all these items fit together."

"Does it anywhere in the packet say 'Ask your parent for help?' I doubt it. You are smart enough to figure it out."

"But…"

"No buts… Just do it."

A salty taste flooded Bella's mouth.

And then Bella was looking out a car window. The scene outside the window was wintery. The branches of the evergreens were heavy with snow, and the pedestrians on the neighborhood sidewalks were bundled up with stocking caps, scarves, and oversized coats. The scene inside the window was heated. The vents blasted hot air upon the two passengers, one driving and the other riding. The discourse was more of an interrogation than a conversation.

"Can you explain to me *why*"—the weight of the word was so heavy it nearly crushed the receiver—"you were not Clara in tonight's performance of *The Nutcracker*? You led me to believe that you were Clara. I was so proud, I told all my friends, and now… now I am a laughingstock. Do you understand how you humiliated me? You are not good enough to even dance the Sugar Plum Fairy."

Bella could not see the face of the woman shouting in the driver's seat, but each word pushed her further away from the mirror. She couldn't imagine how the young girl of eleven was not crumbling.

"Why did you not tell me you were one of the snowflakes? A snowflake! I can't believe it."

The young girl never uttered a word.

Finally, she was back in the girl's room. The pointe shoes hung from a hook on a bright pink wall. The room was adorned with trophies. Trophies that marked the accomplishments in ballet, dance line, gymnastics, and various musical successes. In the spaces not covered by trophies were pictures and posters of dancers, musicians, and a couple of photographs of teenage girls being teenage girls. Six American Girls dolls rested peacefully atop the bedspread. The accompanying books, detailing the story of the doll, lined the shelves next to the bed. Not a single thing appeared out of place.

The room reminded Bella of something she might see in *Better Homes and Gardens* showcasing the ideal teenage girl's room. The title might be "The Room Every Girl Deserves."

As she surveyed the room for any evidence that the space had been occupied and wasn't just a markup for a photo shoot, the door pushed inward. The person who entered wasn't a teenager, but an adult. Although Bella could not see the person's face, even after they sat on the edge of the bed.

The woman reached out and selected McKenna Brooks, the 2012 Girl of the Year doll. McKenna was a budding gymnast. The doll disappeared from Bella's sight as it was brought to the woman's chest. The woman began to rock back and forth, holding the doll deep in her chest. Bella sat transfixed trying to imagine the source of the woman's pain. There was no question. The woman was overwhelmed with grief. Until that moment she was not bothered by the fact that she hadn't seen the woman's face. Bella assumed the woman was Mama, but Bella couldn't be sure unless she heard the woman speak.

The woman never spoke. An hour after entering the room, McKenna was placed next to the other five dolls. The woman stood and straightened the bedspread. She walked to the center of the room, stopped, and slowly turned a complete 360 degrees. She then stepped through the doorway and pulled the door shut behind her. The air created by the door swinging shut struck the pointe shoes so that they moved slightly. First to the right and then left.

The mirror went dark, and Bella was left staring at her reflection.

She removed the pointe shoes and returned them to the north wall. She scanned the building to make sure all the lights were off and then stepped through the doorway and pulled the door shut behind her.

Chapter 23

Thanksgiving and the days following offered Bella little relief from the abrupt end to the image of the ballerina and the young girl's mama. She was haunted by not knowing any details. What was the girl's name? Who was Mama? Most frightening, what happened to the young girl? Where was she?

It didn't help that Brent was traveling with his family to visit his brother and sister-in-law. Texting wasn't the same as being able to discuss matters face-to-face.

A momentary reprieve from agonizing arrived late Sunday evening as Brent strolled into the house. Brent's brother had already gathered a few pieces of information on Marge. He hoped, although he could not promise, that within a week or two, he would be able to provide a full account. As for her dad, the obvious search methods all hit a wall, but not to worry, there were the less than obvious routes available. Nothing to report on George.

Bella threw her arms around him and snuggled against his body. She was excited to receive the news of his brother's efforts, but it was Brent's presence that brought comfort. Until that moment, she did not realize the full extent of how much she missed him.

He spoke of the six-hour car ride, of eating turkey and stuffing, sweet potatoes, mashed potatoes, and cranberries on a plastic plate with plastic utensils. In elaborate detail, he described how his extended family members, including grandparents and aunts and uncles with their children, all crammed into a two-bedroom house designed for two people. He laughed as he described how everyone took a seat for the Thanksgiving meal.

"Folding chairs were set up everywhere including in the doorway to the bathroom. We made Grandpa sit there since his bladder is weak, his prostate is large, and he can't hear."

As Bella joined in the laughter, part of her wished she had accepted Brent's offer to make the trip and meet his extended family. But she had not wanted to leave her mom and grandma home alone. Plus, she had agreed to help Marge with the store. And then, of course, there were the ballet shoes.

Intermission to the disquieting acts of worry ended abruptly with the thought of the shoes. Several images flashed before her, and she contemplated sharing with Brent the young girl whom she met and the faceless woman, Mama, who troubled her. Her contemplation did not result in action. Instead, she swallowed hard and proceeded to describe her Thanksgiving and returning to work on Friday.

It was not the first time she withheld something from Brent. She hoped it would be the last, but she fully realized that was wishful thinking. Shoving the thought downward, she promised herself that she would invite him to witness the next pair of shoes.

Chapter 24

The two weeks before Christmas Eve saw Bella working five days a week. Two of Marge's full-time employees were unable to work. One had pneumonia and was hospitalized, and the other fell and broke her leg and also required a stint in the hospital. Bella's schedule would have been all six days that the Rerun Thrift Store was open if it had not been for wrestling.

Brent had decided that he was not going to defend his state championship wrestling title his senior year. His body was beat up from the football season and needed time to mend. He prioritized improving his GPA and class rank over increasing his undefeated numbers. And most importantly, he decided that spending time with Bella was more important than pushing some guy's face into the mat before flipping him over and pinning him.

But Bella convinced him that he could delay his start to the season and use the time to let his body heal and his academic performance improve. She also promised him that she would attend at least one match a week and make sure every Sunday afternoon was highlighted on her personal calendar as *Brent Time*. As a result, Brent was wrestling, and work became Bella's second home.

Due to being short-staffed, Marge's demeanor was less tranquil than normal with the passing of each day. She developed a nervous tick that increased the speed at which she spoke. The volume of her voice intensified a decibel or two, which meant there were no private conversations, not even those that might occur behind closed doors.

There was also something different about the way Marge spoke. Inexplicably, it sounded familiar to Bella. Unfortunately not familiar enough that she could identify when or where she heard it previously.

The Saturday before Christmas, the Rerun Thrift Store smelled like a bakery. It was a tradition Marge started many years earlier. An assortment of Christmas goodies was available for all patrons along with coffee, tea, and apple cider. It was her way of thanking the community for supporting the business as well as reaching out to those who would not have an opportunity to taste the holiday season. The event grew each year to the point where attendance was part of many families' Christmas tradition. It included bringing goodies to share and gifts to be delivered to those without a home. It was quite a spectacle as bags of items were carried in and bags of items were carried out. The standing joke was that this was the one day each year that the store needed a revolving door.

Bella smiled as she watched groups of people, who any other time would have avoided the other, stood side by side and spoke with each other. Childhood memories floated through the store. Memories of baking cookies with Mom. Of trimming the Christmas tree. Of wrapping gifts. Of singing carols. Of attending candlelight worship services. Of playing with a new game or toy. Of playing with the box in which the new game or toy came. Of going to see Santa. Of feeling a sense of loss when it was all over. Bella smiled because she too knew these memories. Bella smiled because this was community.

It was nearly eleven when the building held only Marge and Bella and the only space left in need of attention was the bathroom. Bella told Marge that she would finish the bathroom and then lock up.

"Thank you, Bella. I will take you up on that offer. It has been a terribly long day, and my head is pounding. But before I leave, please come join me for a cup of tea and one of my special Christmas cookies."

The table placed along the north wall that earlier held rows and rows of goodies now supported a single plate with two very unique-looking cookies. Reading the bewilderment in Bella's eyes, Marge proceeded to describe the cookies before Bella reached the table.

"They sort of look like a croissant, don't they? But I assure you, the only similarity is in the shape. They are walnut vanilla cookies, rolled in powdered sugar. It is a recipe from the old country. My grandmother called them Vanillekipferl; that's Romanian for vanilla walnut cookie. They are not that difficult to make, but we had them only at Christmas because the ingredients were not always available."

With a mouth full, Bella mumbled, "They are delish."

Marge inquired if Bella had a favorite holiday food or tradition that was sacred and therefore practiced every year. Bella described how when she was little the entire family would assemble at Grandpa and Grandma's house. Santa would come and each child would sit on his lap. She started to reminisce about how she asked Santa for a Barbie car, pink in color when she saw them behind Marge's right ear.

A white pair of high-top basketball shoes. But not just any pair of basketball shoes.

With her phone in hand, her fingers raced across the keys, searching for the correct name of the shoes and the year they were first released. Bella wasn't sure but they appeared to be an authentic pair and not a retro-released pair.

Marge watched and then grew concerned. It wasn't like Bella to place her phone between the two of them when they were speaking. "Everything okay?"

Without looking up, Bella spoke, "Yes, just give me one second and I'll explain."

Marge took a sip of her tea and sat back to wait.

Still staring at her phone with her fingers still moving across the keys, Bella asked, "Marge, do you know what you have on the wall behind you?"

Not moving, Marge responded, "Shoes, dear. Lots of pairs of shoes."

"No, you have a single pair of shoes like no other."

"Really?" Marge turned, first to the right and then left studying the wall in both directions. "And which pair might that be?"

For the first time, Bella looked up from the phone as she spoke. "The white shoes."

Not looking to confirm the exact number, Marge said, "Bella, there are at least fifteen different pairs of white shoes. Be more specific."

"To your right, third row up, high tops."

Marge continued to look at Bella as she spoke. "Oh yeah. Just arrived. Very clean. Didn't need to be scrubbed."

Looking at the shoes, Bella asked, "Do you know what they are?"

"Nikes, I believe."

Smiling like a kid receiving their first bike, Bella said, "They are so much more than Nikes."

Marge turned, looked at the shoes for a brief moment, and then turned back to Bella and asked, "How is it that you know so much about basketball shoes? I haven't seen you wearing them."

"Brent…"

"Say no more."

Turning her phone so the screen was visible, Bella showed Marge a picture of a similar pair of shoes. Marge read the eBay ad out loud. "Nike Air Jordan Concord XI was released in 1995. White patent leather top with translucent bottoms. $1.000.00."

As Bella pulled the phone back, Marge asked, "You don't seriously think those are an original pair of shoes from 1995, do you?"

Bella scrolled through story after story concerning the shoes and shared, "I doubt they were purchased in 1995, but I do believe they are a pair from the '90s. Without additional documentation, you probably can't get a thousand for them, but I would guess several hundred bucks."

"Bella, who is going to pay a couple hundred bucks in this store for a pair of basketball shoes?"

"I don't know, Marge. There were plenty of people in here today who could have afforded the shoes. I'm just surprised no one…" Bella stopped herself and thought for a moment before she continued. "Marge, when did you put the shoes on the wall?"

"Oh, I didn't get them out until after we closed. I was just so busy I forgot about them."

Bella just smiled.

* * *

"Brent? I know it's late, but Marge just left and if possible, you need to come down to the store and see these shoes. I mean… well, you just need to see them."

"Are you planning to put them on?" It was more important to know if she planned to put them on than what type of shoe she had.

Without a moment's hesitation, Bella responded, "You bet I am."

By the time Brent arrived, the bathroom was clean, and Bella was admiring the Air Jordans. It was obvious they had been worn, but they were in good condition.

Brent identified the shoes immediately. "You gotta be kidding. Someone gave these shoes to the store to be sold? Do you know how much they are worth?"

"Yeah. Well, sort of."

"Did Marge have anything to do with the shoes?"

Bella's shoulders rose as she responded. "That's the thing, I don't know. If she did, she was very subtle, even sneaky about it." Bella went on to describe how Marge invited her to share a cookie and how they sat at the table. She ended with, "I don't know how she could have forgotten to display the shoes on a day like this. It doesn't make sense, except…" Bella paused.

"Except what?" The words leaped from his mouth as he anticipated something significant to be forthcoming.

Slowly Bella spoke, "Except Marge has been stressed with Christmas and being short-staffed, so… it's possible… that she did forget."

Brent's shoulders dropped. It wasn't the response he expected. Clearing his throat, he asked, "You are still going to try them on, right?"

She nodded her head twice and loosened the strings. Her foot probably would have slid right in the size 13 shoe, but it was a habit. As she worked her nails under the strings her thoughts drifted back.

"You know, when I was in fifth grade, I wanted to play basketball."

"Why didn't you?"

She thought as she set one shoe aside and picked up the other. "I think it was for a number of reasons. I wasn't fond of the coach. Did you ever have Mr. Drill Sergeant for Phy Ed?"

With a laugh, Brent answered. "Oh yeah, he loved me. He liked anyone who went all out during class."

"Yeah, and he also liked the girls?"

"No way, Drill Sergeant?"

"Oh, yeah! He would stare at us and whenever possible he would brush up against us."

"Okay, so there was the coach. What were the other reasons for not going out for basketball?"

"I doubted my ability. I knew some of the girls had been playing summer rec and were good. But honestly, the main reason, and don't laugh, promise?"

"I promise. Scout's honor."

"Too bad you're not a scout." Bella finished with the second shoe and set it next to the other one. "Showering."

Brent looked confused. "Showering? I don't understand."

"At the end of practice, all girls were required to take a shower."

"Yeah, so?"

"Showering in front of other girls, in fifth grade? Not gonna happen."

"Sorry, but I need a bit more. What's the big deal?"

"Fifth grade, Brent!"

Shaking his head all he could do was repeat her words. "Fifth grade."

"Do you know what happens or doesn't happen to girls in fifth grade?"

"Obviously not, otherwise I would know what the hell you are talking about."

"Maturity! Boobs, pubic hair, period."

Brent didn't need to say a word. The color of his face said it all.

"Wasn't that an issue for boys?"

Brent started to chuckle, "Nope, other than a few whisps of hair, there weren't any boobs or any blood."

"Stop it. You're just being gross now."

"I was trying to be funny."

"Well, you failed."

"So what was the problem? You weren't developed or you were?"

With her head tilted, and her brow wrinkled, she answered the question as though it didn't require a response. "Look at me now. You really think the issue was I was too developed? Come on."

"I don't care what you say. I think you are just fine."

Bella smiled but let him know it was a serious thing for a fifth grader. "You say that now, but I doubt that's what you would have said back then."

He leaned in and just before he kissed her, he said, "I guess we'll never know."

After the kiss, Bella got the last word on the subject, "I guess we won't."

Looking at the shoes next to Bella, Brent said, "You didn't play basketball as a fifth grader. Maybe this is your big chance to play ball. Maybe those shoes belonged to a basketball star."

"There's one way to find out." Both feet dropped into the shoes, and the laces were pulled tight.

Chapter 25

The shoes were not even visible. They were tucked inside a gym bag that rested between the driver and the passenger. At the moment, the driver wasn't driving the vehicle but had just carefully steered onto the shoulder and placed the car in park. Red and blue lights intermittently struck the driver's eyes as they reflected off the rear-view mirror.

Reaching for his driver's license, in response to the request from the officer who stood next to the car door, the driver's eyes noticed, in the rear-view mirror, the eyes of the two passengers in the back seat. He saw fear. It seemed unwarranted since he was driving; he knew he had not violated any laws.

With the driver's license in hand, the officer directed the beam of light from his flashlight into the interior of the car. First to the passenger in the front and then toward the two in the back. His words sounded friendly enough, "Where you boys headed tonight?"

The driver answered, "On our way home from basketball practice."

The officer tilted the flashlight to the driver's license. "Says here your address is not even from this city. You headed all the way across the state."

"No, sir. We are college students attending State University. We have an apartment across town."

"Rich boys, yeah? Got your own apartment?"

"No, sir, we all are scholarship players."

"Don't go getting smart with me, boy."

"No, sir."

"Damn right, 'no sir.' I think you boys should all step outside the car."

A voice from the back rang out, "What did we do wrong, officer?"

"What you are doing wrong is you are not getting out of the car. Now move it."

Slowly the doors opened and the four boys, all over six feet five inches, stood on the side of the road.

"Here is how this is going to go. You all can save yourself a lot of trouble and hand over the drugs, or I can call for a dog and we'll let him rip the inside of your car to shreds."

The driver spoke up, "Sir, we don't have any drugs. I assure you."

"What do you take me for, a fool? I smelled it the moment I passed your rear fender. Which, by the way, has a taillight out."

The passenger seated in the front seat poked the driver in the ribs and shook his head, but it wasn't enough to stop the driver from speaking.

"I don't mean to disagree with you sir, but I know that the taillight is not broken."

"Well, let's have a look. Come with me and we'll check it out."

As the driver and the officer reached the rear of the car, the flashlight struck the red plastic and it shattered. "See, what did I tell you? A broken rear taillight. Now, you boys are going to hand over the drugs, or do I call in the dog?"

The four of them looked at each other and each, very slowly, barely noticeably, shook their heads.

Back in line with the other three, the driver said again, "Sorry, sir, but we don't have any drugs."

"We'll just see."

Thirty-five minutes later another patrol car pulled up and from the back seat came a dog.

"Last chance, boys. Let me assure you, it goes a lot easier if you hand it over as opposed to us finding it. Easier, as in the punishment is less harsh."

The four never moved. They just stared at the two officers and the dog.

"Go ahead Joe, turn Mac loose. I already warned them that Mac might tear up the car."

The dog first worked the outside of the car. His tail was going ninety miles an hour. This was sheer enjoyment for the dog. With the driver's door open, Mac's head disappeared, and he sniffed the dashboard, and then the gym bag that held the shoes. Within a matter of seconds, his entire body was in the front seat pulling the officer halfway inside the car trying to keep a hold of the leash.

Effortlessly, the dog leaped into the back seat and sniffed every inch of the floor, the seat, the fabric on the roof, and along the back window. With dog drool covering the seats, it appeared Mac didn't hit on anything. The car was clean.

The office stepped forward and informed Joe that he would open the back door so Mac would not have to climb back over the seat to exit. "Joe, hold Mac tight for a second. I'll open the door. Hand me the leash, and you can slide out."

As the door opened the officer reached into the back seat to take control of Mac. As the officer stepped back outside the car, Mac went crazy. His front paws ripped into the leather of the back seat. Joe quickly reached around the open car door, took the leash, and commanded Mac to heel. Mac perched like a bird on the edge of the seat with his nose pointing to the spot where his paws had been digging.

The four basketball players standing beside the car knew that something had been planted in the car by the officer. Yet none of them said a word. They merely watched as a baggy was pulled from the crease of the seat.

"My, my, what do we have here? What do you think, Joe? Feels like more than 50 grams. We're talking almost two ounces. Felony, isn't it?"

With both Mac and Joe standing outside the car, Joe said, "Looks like it. Bag it and we'll weigh it when we get back to the station. I'll put Mac back in the car and call for another car. We'll need a second to transport all four of them."

"Hey man," one of the passengers from the back seat spoke. "We all know you planted that. What's the deal?"

"Deal?" The officer laughed. "There is no deal, boy. You had your chance, and you blew it. By the way, boys, I wouldn't try using the "planting drugs" story. That never works. It only means you are guilty."

* * *

As Brent watched Bella, it was disconcerting to witness how labored her breathing had become. He was worried that she was under duress. Several times her body pulled back away from the mirror, and she struck the wall behind her. He was not able to discern if she was a witness to the events unfolding in the mirror or experiencing the events. What he did conclude was that something other than a basketball game was transpiring. There was a point when Bella's entire body dropped. As an athlete, Brent recognized the body language as a sign of defeat, of giving up. It was the moment when an opponent could smell victory and stepped up and took control.

Feeling the weight of defeat, total abandonment of any will or desire to live, Bella watched as the once touted NBA prospect, compared to the likes of Kevin Garrett, was shoved into a sterile cell with the heavy metal door sliding shut. When his mother came to visit him at the county jail, before he was transported to a state prison to serve his sentence for possession of an illegal substance, they sat across from one another at a conference table. Between them was a plexiglass divider to keep any physical contact from occurring. As the time was about to expire for their visit, the question was finally asked.

"What should I do with your basketball shoes?"

"My shoes? Mom, you do know that I am not guilty, right? No matter what the jury decided, I'm innocent."

"Yes, yes, I believe you. But that doesn't change the fact that you are in… I just wanted to know what to do with the shoes."

"Put them back in the box and set them in my closet."

"Are you sure, I mean…"

"Please, Mom."

The scene changed abruptly; it was initially difficult for Bella to determine what was before her. It appeared to be a small room. Bella was unable to smell anything, but she assumed if she could, the odor would be foul. She imagined something like a mixture of human sweat, cooking grease, and smoke. From the narrow stream of sunlight that passed between a small slit in the window coverings, possibly blankets, a small coffee table was visible. On the table was an ashtray spilling over with cigarette butts, three, maybe four plates with bits of uneaten food sticking over the edges, and a newspaper folded in half. Above the table was a single light bulb that hung three feet from the ceiling. Without the bulb lit, it was too dark to read the newspaper in hopes of establishing a date. Without any additional evidence, Bella was left questioning why this scene covered the entire mirror.

She sat quietly and waited. There had to be a reason for this scene to appear in the mirror. She told herself to be patient. She hoped that eventually her eyes would adjust to the darkness, and she would be able to find an answer.

On impulse, her body jerked as the single light bulb sprang to life less than a second after a clicking sound was heard. There wasn't time for her brain to prepare her eyes for the brightness that momentarily blinded her. Blinking her eyelids several times she slowly adapted, and the one-room apartment came into focus. The gentleman responsible for the blindness took a seat on a threadbare couch next to the coffee table and immediately put a flame to the end of a cigarette. His body fell back against the couch as he propped his feet on the table. There were the shoes. The 1995 Nike Air Jordan Concord XI shoes. They appeared as new as the pair upon her own feet.

Watching as he nursed the cigarette, she concluded that, despite having aged and carrying an additional twenty pounds, this was the young man who drove the car. This was the young man who asked his mother to put his shoes in his closet. This was the young man, now a much older man, who was sent to prison for a crime he did not commit.

The newspaper next to the basketball shoes was now readable. The bold letters all in caps read, "FORMER OFFICER CONV..." The remainder of the headline and the date were laid face down on the table. Without forethought Bella's right hand left her side as she reached out. Her efforts were futile as she was merely an observer.

Her brain worked to complete the partially revealed word. Multiple options bubbled up. Convalescent. Convened. Converted. Conveyed. Convinced. Convoluted.

The former athlete's foot struck the paper and pushed it from the tabletop as he leaned forward to flick ashes onto the heap of butts filling the ashtray. With the cigarette returned to the corner of his mouth, he reached for the paper on the floor and carelessly tossed it back on the table. It landed unfolded enabling Bella to read the entire headline, "FORMER OFFICER CONVICTED OF PLANTING EVIDENCE."

Her eyes lifted to the top of the page, November 4, 2009.

Squinting, she was able to read most of the article that followed. The article described how the former county officer was found guilty of planting evidence against four basketball players from State University a decade earlier. The four were found guilty of possessing and transporting an illegal substance for the purpose of selling the substance. As a result, the four were sentenced to prison. Through the tireless efforts of citizens who worked to uncover a pattern of such behavior by the county deputy over a period of twenty years, his criminal actions were exposed. It was discovered that he targeted these four gentlemen after he lost a substantial amount of money when State University upset a top-ranked opponent. An undercover sting operation under the direction of the Bureau of Criminal Apprehension revealed how the officer in question had been blackmailing victims for years by planting evidence with the promise not to arrest the individual in exchange for money. The four basketball players refused to succumb to blackmail.

Witnessing the spent cigarette added to the pile, Bella tried to determine if it was weeks, months, or possibly even years after the newspaper had been published that now saw the driver of the car and owner of the shoes in the one-room apartment. Searching the room for any clues, her efforts were interrupted as music and the lyrics from the song *Unbelievable* rang out. Startled, she jerked back, unsure of the source of the song until a phone appeared from the front pants pocket.

"How you doin', man?" The phone set to the speaker allowed Bella to hear the gentleman's voice.

"I'm still trying to comprehend how Scotty and Mike didn't make it out of prison." With the phone perched on his thigh, he pulled another cigarette from the pack as he spoke.

"Man, I can't believe you never heard about their deaths."

"I can't either. The communication pipeline inside is unbelievable. It adds to my suspension that neither of them committed suicide."

Oh, man, there's no doubt. Neither of them would end it. You know Scotty. He hated pain. From what I heard, he died a slow painful death. There's no way. And Mike?" The voice from the phone paused. "His old man will hunt him down in the afterlife and do a number on him. He knew it, too. Nope, those boys were killed because they knew something. Something big."

"Any idea what it was about?"

"No. Hey, and even if I did, I ain't talkin'. You know the arm reaches beyond the bars."

"Yeah, I know, but…"

"But nothing, man. We ain't bringing them back. It's time we just get on with life."

"Right, easier said than done." The words were delivered with a bit of laughter.

"We're not felons. Our record is wiped clean. What was the word they used… expunged?"

"That might be, but no one's knocking down my door to hire me."

"You still sitting on that worn-out, old couch?"

Before answering, he leaned forward to drop the stained filtered butt to the pile which sent the phone crashing to the floor. With the screen facing the grungy carpet the voice was muffled, "Hey, what happened? You okay?"

With the phone in hand, he explained how it slid from his leg. He welcomed the distraction as it offered a diversion from having to address his living arrangement. He knew his mom would allow him to live with her, but at the age of thirty-two, he wasn't about to move back home. He couldn't do that.

What ate at his spirit was how, in the blink of an eye, his whole world crumbled, and the weight of the rumble was now exacerbated by the death of his friends. How was it that knowledge, knowing something, could terminate two lives? He had bought into the argument that knowledge was power, and therefore knowledge gave life, it protected life, it was life. His entire existence, whether playing basketball, studying pre-med, or just kicking back with video games, was about securing knowledge. Yet, knowledge did not bring justice. Knowledge did not wield the power necessary to right the wrong. Knowledge in the hands of corrupt individuals, of selfish egotistical maniacs, of vindictive crusaders compounds the depth of the injustice.

Bella understood that the man before her in the mirror wore the Nike Air Jordan Concord XI as a mockery against everything he once deemed important. He took up sanctuary in a one-room apartment because he found himself in a no-win situation. In order to get back into the "game" of life, he needed to participate in the very thing he identified as part of the problem. Knowledge. Or, at least, the knowledge valued by those in power. Knowledge was power only if it was the certified and condoned knowledge by the powerful. Bella could feel the turmoil that rolled within his body. He became his own worst enemy. Or… was he…?

She stopped herself when she realized that she was judging him with the knowledge he was questioning. Was he his own worst enemy? Or was the enemy those who capitalized upon his demise? Those who would continue to profit at his expense because he would always be viewed as an ex-con?

She watched as he lit yet another cigarette and she felt like a hypocrite. It felt as though the end of the match used to light the cigarette touched the tip of her nose. Her face became hot, and she felt nauseous. She had tried to present herself to the world as a nonconformist. As someone who wasn't about fads, someone with a moral compass.

Someone who understood the difference between fairness and justice. Someone who would one day work for peace and justice. But sitting on the floor in the dressing room staring at the mirror, the revelation was brighter than the bulb overhead. Her shoes were no different than the Nike Air Jordans.

The Doc Martens she wore day in and day out, meant to be a symbol of rebellion, were nothing more than profit for the manufacturer. Knowledge is power but only for a few!

It could just as easily be her seated on the ragged couch, smoking cigarette after cigarette.

The thought that someday someone might slide their feet into *her* shoes, and they would experience her hypocrisy ripped at her cord. She couldn't breathe… there wasn't enough air… the image in the mirror began to fade… she understood… she needed to remove those basketball shoes… no…she needed to destroy them… she understood… the shoes represented everything that destroyed the life of one young basketball player… she understood… the truth of the message delivered in the shoes… she understood… the soul of the shoes.

Chapter 26

"Bella! Bella! What in God's name are you doing to those basketball shoes? They are worth…" The words echoed through the entire store as Brent shouted at Bella as she laid a knife to the shoes.

"They are worthless." She cried with tears flowing. "They destroyed one life. I will not permit them to destroy another."

He reached for the back of her hand carving at the shoe tops. Attempting to lift the knife away from the shoes, he said, "That's crazy! Shoes can't destroy a person's life."

Without looking at him she dipped her shoulder to increase her strength, but he was too strong. The blade did not slash the leather again. Dropping the knife beneath his claw-like grip, she replied, "You are so naïve. You don't get it."

"What are you talking about? What don't I get?"

"Just forget it. You would never understand."

"Bella." His voice was soft and gentle. "You can't say I don't understand if you haven't shared anything with me. You say you trust me, yet you pull away whenever you are scared. That's not fair."

"You haven't experienced what I have. There is no way you can understand." The pace of her words was quick and filled with passion. Her fists were clenched as she spoke.

He remained silent for several minutes and waited for her breathing to calm. When he spoke, he again spoke softly. "It's more than the shoes, isn't it? It's also what you see in the mirror."

She looked at him with total surprise. Eager to hear his answer, she blurted out the question, "Did you see him in the mirror?"

"No. I didn't see anything. But as I watched you, I saw how your body moved in response to whatever it was you witnessed in the mirror."

"Yes." She leaned in closer to him as she spoke. "It all seems so real. It is as though each person is right there, within arm's length. But they are not."

"What is it about the mirror?"

"It's the place of truth."

"Truth?" He said it a second time. "Truth?" And then slowly confessed, "I don't understand."

"It's the place we hope to find perfection reflected back at us, but what we get is truth. Truth in the form of all the imperfections of who we are. Truth in the form of decisions gone bad. Truth in the crumbling of relationships. Truth in dreams never reached. Truth in the naked reality of who we are and who we are not!" She looked directly at him to deliver the final statement. She spoke each word slowly, "The mirror never lies." Allowing the truth to penetrate both their ears, she finally added, "The mirror, that mirror," she pointed to the dressing room, "reveals the soul of those whose shoes I wear. I feel it with my own feet and see it with my own eyes."

He wrapped his arms around her shoulders and held her tight. There was nothing he could say that wouldn't sound trite. So, he kept silent.

Chapter 27

Christmas came and went. It was enjoyable but for a different reason than when Bella was a child. She had reached the age where it was more rewarding to watch another open a gift shared than to count the presents bearing one's own name. She had spent time Christmas Eve and morning with her mom and grandma, and the afternoon of Christmas Day with Brent and his parents. What brought the greatest anticipation was the day after Christmas when Brent's brother Robert and his family would arrive. Bella was hopeful that he would bring news of Marge and her father.

It began with awkward introductions and traditional small talk as everyone patiently waited for the noon meal to be served. Brent's parents invited Bella and her mom to join them so that the immediate family members might all meet one another. By the middle of the afternoon, Bella was exhausted from playing with Brent's niece and nephew and a bit frustrated that there hadn't been a free moment to speak in private with Robert.

Sensing that Bella was anxious, Brent whispered, "My brother wants to take us out for breakfast in the morning. At that time, he'll share an update on Marge and hopefully something about your dad and maybe even George. Okay?"

Playfully shoving Brent aside, Bella said, "Of course, any time works for me, I hadn't really even given it any thought."

Smiling, Brent said, "Whatever you say."

* * *

The waitress's order pad held the breakfast wishes of the three, as Robert directed his gaze to Bella, and asked, "Are you familiar with Boxing Day?"

She hesitated for a moment considering the relevance of the question. "It was yesterday, right? The day after Christmas."

"That's correct," Robert responded very matter-of-factly.

Yesterday, Robert was Brent's brother. He was a husband, a father of two, a person Bella felt comfortable to engage in conversation. A person one was not intimidated by or guarded in the choice of words used. That was not the case seated in the tiny café located several blocks off Main Street. A café that served a regular crowd of customers, except for Saturday mornings when people drove miles and waited in line to experience a bit of Americana, 1950s style.

The gentleman seated across from Bella and Brent fully resembled the secret service man that he was. Beyond the edge of professionalism, there was also a sense that Robert was completely in control not only of their private conversation but the entire room. Bella imagined that if she asked Robert to close his eyes and describe everyone and everything in the café, he could and would perform the feat with certainty and confidence. As a result, before he could ask another question, she added, "That's all I know."

"Don't feel bad. Most people don't know anything about Boxing Day. And I suppose, it's not really surprising since in the States we don't celebrate or honor the tradition. The history, however, is rather interesting. I won't cover all the details but get to the point of why it's called Boxing Day. In the early Eighteen Hundreds, the rich folks gave their servants the day off after Christmas. Since these wealthy families would host large parties on Christmas Day, servants were required to work and attend to the needs of the guests. Therefore, the day after they were permitted to relax and celebrate their own Christmases. In addition to being granted a day off from work, they also would receive a box of goodies from their wealthy employer. The tradition quickly expanded beyond just the servants tied to a household to include all the poor. The rich folks would box up items, and the boxes were distributed to the poor who had the day off from their labors. Since the tradition originated in England, over time it was incorporated into all of Great Britain's colonies."

Brent sat and listened as patiently as Bella and spoke first when Robert finished. "That's a nice history lesson, but what the hell does that have to do with Marge, George, or Bella's dad?"

Without changing his expression, Robert responded, "Did I ever suggest it did?"

"No. But you always have some point or connection to your stories. Otherwise you don't tell them. And don't say, 'It's a nice story related to the season.'"

"Little brother, I'm impressed. You are learning." For a moment, there was a crack in Robert's demeanor, and he again seemed human.

"Little brother? You just wait until we get home, and we'll see who the little brother is. You'll be begging me to let you up."

"So you…"

"Boys, seriously. Am I the only adult at the table?" Bella spoke playfully, but also she was serious. She had been patient long enough. It was time to hear what had been discovered. She added, just as three plates heaped with food arrived at their table, "You boys can finish this childish flexing of muscle when you get home. I want to hear what, if anything, you have learned."

Swallowing the first fork full of scrambled eggs and washing it down with a mouthful of dark rich coffee, Robert placed his elbows on the table with his chin resting atop his folded hands and began. "Brent is correct, there is a connection, albeit rather loose. We don't necessarily need Boxing Day because, well, we have places like the Rerun Thrift Store where those less fortunate are able to purchase items for little or nothing."

Bella jumped in. "Are you saying that Marge at one time practiced Boxing Day or was on the receiving end of the day?"

"No, not really. But I think she totally understands the concept. I believe that is her motivation behind the store. Or I should say, one of the reasons. Her story is actually quite detailed with several twists and turns."

"I want to hear it all, and don't leave any details out." Bella pushed her plate forward as though making room for the details.

Robert, directing his attention to the food, said, as he raised his fork balancing three layers of pancakes dripping with maple syrup, "May I inquire why? What's behind your desire to know her story?"

Bella and Brent looked at one another. They needed to decide just how much to tell Robert. What did he need to know? Brent nodded slightly and waited for Bella to take the lead. This was her story after all.

She took a sip of orange juice to give herself an additional moment to carefully order the words. "Marge has been a very patient employer. I might even go so far as to say she is a friend. A friend who has taken an interest in me and my life. Yet also an adult friend with clear boundaries. It's not like she presses me to tell her things or that she tells me personal things. In fact, sometimes…" She paused for a moment and looked at Brent before continuing. "Most of the time, I don't fully grasp the point of our conversations. It's only hours or days later that I understand what she was saying." With both hands raised in front of her, as though waiting to receive a gift, she finished her reply to Robert. "I want to know more about her story so that I might understand better."

The waitress returned with a pot of coffee and filled Robert's cup and asked if everything was okay. As she moved to the next table, Robert nodded twice and said, "I think what I have learned might help you."

He smiled as though wanting Bella to know the details he was about to provide were being delivered not only from a Secret Service man but also from someone she could trust. He began with a question. "What do you know about ballet?"

Bella fell back against the chair and looked at Brent. The color from her face drained, and she appeared like a lifeless body in a casket.

Brent reached for her hand and held it tight. He whispered, "It's okay. It's okay."

Robert's eyes shifted back and forth between the two across the table. His confusion at what he was witnessing told him there was a whole lot more to this situation than either his brother or Bella shared. Waiting for the two to gather themselves, Robert sat motionless. Finally, he asked, "Talk to me, what's triggering you about ballet?"

Leaning forward as though trying to get the blood flowing through her body again, she spoke in a whisper. "First, you tell me how ballet is connected with Marge and I'll..." She stopped for a second, turned to look at Brent, and then finished, "We'll tell you about ballet."

Robert pulled a small notepad from his back pocket and flipped through numerous pages. Locating the page he desired, he spoke. "Melisandre Lupu, known to you as Marge Wolfe, was born in 1965 in Sibiu, Romania, in the heart of Transylvania."

Hearing the word *Transylvania* brought forth a response from Brent and Bella. Both, as though following a director's cue, sighed and shook their heads in unison.

Without stopping, Robert continued. "She is an only child. Her parents were educated."

Bella interrupted, "Were educated? Are you intentionally speaking in the past tense?"

Looking up only for a second, he said, "Yes, but I'll get to that."

Looking back at the notepad, he continued. "Her parents were educated. Mom was a poet. Most of her work was political in nature, although often cleverly hidden in the text. Her father was a musician who taught music at Gheorghe Lazar High School in Sibiu, which is a highly touted academic school. He too was an activist who spoke out against the government."

He paused and directed his attention to Bella and Brent before he drifted from his notes. "In case you are not familiar with Romanian history, when Marge was growing up, they were a communist country supported and controlled by the Soviet Union. Free speech in any form was not a protected right. Due to a number of high-profile defections in Romania and Russia, the controlling grip from the government tightened. People needed to report a list of all their items. Long lines waiting to purchase food became a common sight. The conditions were harsh. The one thing that saved the family from exile was Marge."

Bella straightened as she echoed her employer's name, "Marge? She couldn't have been much more than fifteen or sixteen."

"You are exactly right. The government, or I should say the Securitate, known as the secret police, were willing to tolerate a few minor indiscretions from the family because of her skills. She was an up-and-coming ballerina star. She was dancing with the Romanian National Ballet Company."

Bella nodded several times. "It's all starting to make sense. Or at least, some of it."

Robert took the opportunity to take several more bites of the eggs, now getting cold, and drain his cup of coffee. Signaling for the waitress to bring more coffee, he asked Bella, "You want to share now, or you want me to continue?"

"Please, continue. It might make telling my story easier once I hear everything."

He didn't start until he had a chance to swallow several sips of hot coffee.

"In early 1983, Marge's father decided things were becoming too unpredictable in Romania, and it was time to get his family out of the country. He decided that he would first defect and then once safe, he would send for them. His route for leaving the country was to pass into Hungry and make his way to West Germany. Unfortunately, he was caught and returned to Sibiu and was used by the Securitate to demonstrate what happens to anyone trying to leave the country. He was executed. Marge's mom was jailed and eventually sent to prison where she later died. Propaganda quickly circulated that Ms. Lupu, Marge, the rising star of the National Ballet, was not supportive of her parents' lack of loyalty to the government and that she notified the authorities of her parents' actions."

"Propaganda? So you are suggesting that Marge never did those things?" Brent asked.

"The best we can tell, that would be correct. She didn't report them. Her actions a few years later would support that conclusion."

As Robert and Brent discussed how difficult this must have been for an eighteen year-old, Bella's thoughts race back to the images she saw as she wore the pointe shoes. Was it possible that Marge was the young girl? Or did it make more sense that she was the…

Her thoughts were interrupted by Brent who again took her hand and asked, "You okay? You look like you are lost in thought. Were you… back at the store?"

She nodded and looked at Robert without turning her head.

Robert's head turned slightly as though using his right eye to peer more deeply into Bella's soul as he inquired, "Back at the store?"

Pulling her hand free from Brent, she pushed her palm in Robert's direction, signaling she wasn't ready to explain.

He understood and lifted the notepad. "In 1987, Marge successfully defected and made her way to West Germany. She remained there until she was able to raise enough money to make her way to Canada and finally to the United States in 1997."

"It took her ten years to make it to the States?" Brent's question of disbelief revealed just how unaware he was of a refugee's actions and endless turmoil.

"Yes, that journey itself is a whole other story. In 2000, six months pregnant, she landed here in the city and opened the Rerun Thrift Store. A few months later, at the age of thirty-five, she gave birth to a daughter, Clara…"

"Clara?" Bella stared at Robert. "Clara, as in Clara from the Nutcracker?"

The force of Bella's stare drove Robert back slightly before he spoke. "Yes, I guess so. I never thought of the connection, but it makes sense. When Marge defected, she was cast as Clara in The Nutcracker."

Bella leaned against Brent for support as she continued to fit all the pieces together. With her head on his shoulder, she whispered, "The girl, the girl's name was Clara. I wonder why she never used her name?"

Brent tilted his head bringing his mouth next to her ear. "That would mean… the woman was Marge."

"Yes."

Chapter 28

Robert didn't interrupt the conversation across the table. He just sat and listened. He realized that there was a whole other piece to this story, and it was just possible that Bella and Brent might know something that would assist him in putting closure to an open file. A file that was started seven years earlier. A file he stepped into because of following Marge's story.

Waiting patiently to ensure that neither Bella nor Brent was going to say more, Robert spoke. "Care to share with me now what the two of you have been discussing? I have a feeling it is pertinent to Marge's story."

Bella carefully lifted herself off Brent and said, "Not quite yet. Please finish."

Robert cleared his throat. He was struggling with being forced to wear two different hats. As a Secret Service man, he would never have allowed someone to dictate the course of a conversation, but as Brent's brother, this was how family members responded to one another. He concluded the family "hat" needed to stay on.

"Clara, like her mother, took up ballet. She too was a natural. She was carefully being groomed. From those with whom I spoke, those who coached Clara, there was a balancing act employed to offset Marge's role. For an extended period, they went through several coaches, because, as they reported, Clara's mom didn't trust or respect them and demanded that they push Clara harder. Marge, according to everyone with whom I spoke, stated the same thing, Marge was very vocal and forceful."

Bella softly interjected, "Not the Marge you would meet today. At least, not the Marge greeting customers and giving directions to her employees."

"Well, sometimes life has a way of changing people."

It was Bella's turn to cock her head to the left and narrow her focus on Robert's face as she asked, "What do you mean, changing?"

"In 2013, Clara went missing."

Chapter 29

Bella slouched in her chair. She had considered this possibility, but now it was reality. "She went missing in 2013, so the open file you spoke of is a missing person's file, correct?"

"That's correct."

"And there are no leads?"

"Currently, no. Back in 2013, the police followed up on several, but nothing panned out. Is there anything you would like to add?"

She looked at Brent and then down at her hands in her lap. She spoke without looking up. "I promised I would share what I know, but do you mind if we leave? I need some fresh air. The walls are starting to move inward."

"I think that's a great idea."

Following the flow of traffic out of the city, the three sat in silence. Bella and Brent sat beside each other in the back and Robert served as the chauffeur. A few miles past the city limits, traffic thinned and Robert set the cruise.

Glancing up at the rearview mirror, he monitored his passengers as they whispered to one another.

Bella described her predicament. "I feel like I am wearing someone else's shoes, experiencing someone else's story. And then I look down and see it's my shoes that I am wearing. It feels so surreal. Who would ever believe this?"

"You can trust him, Bella. I realize that you just met him yesterday, but..."

Bella squeezed Brent's hand and stopped him. After a moment of staring out the side window at the barren landscape, she said, "It's not about trusting him or you. It's about trusting myself. It's about believing that everything I have experienced was real…" Her breath stopped for a second and she inhaled deeply as she considered the ending to that sentence. "And that somehow, Marge…" She was not ready for the outside world to hear what tumbled about inside her mind. Or perhaps the world was not ready for the truth.

"Robert." She looked at the rearview mirror so that she might see his face as she spoke. "Any idea what happened or where Clara might be?"

Robert met her eyes in the mirror and then looked back at the road as he answered. "The report in the file states that she ran away. Because there has been and continues to be a high degree of sex trafficking recruitment in the city, one theory is prostitution. However, there was no concrete evidence to support that theory and if that was the case, what's surprising is that there is no record of anyone fitting Clara's description being arrested for solicitation." Robert's eyes again met Bella's. "Most of the girls recruited locally end up being shipped off to Atlanta or Dallas. The database on these girls is quite sophisticated so that if she…"

"I had a dream." Bella had decided that rather than try and explain the ballet shoes and what she experienced by placing them on her feet, she would describe the event as a dream. "It seemed so real that I shared it with Brent." She looked at him and smiled.

They were lost in each other's gaze. Robert knew better than to interrupt.

Bella broke free from Brent's captivating allure, looked at the rearview mirror, and continued, "In this dream, I saw an older woman enter a room, a girl's bedroom. There was a pair of pointe shoes hanging from a hook on the wall. On the bed was an American Girl doll that the woman cradled next to her body. That's why we asked you to find out about Marge.

"At the time of the dream did you think the older woman was Marge?" Robert now wore his Secret Service "hat".

"Yes and no. I had no reason to believe it was Marge. I never saw the woman's face. And the voice," after a momentary pause, she repeated herself, "The voice sounded familiar but not exactly like Marge's. Again, this event occurred only after Marge showed me a pair of ballet shoes that came into the Rerun Thrift Store."

"She never said anything about them belonging to her?" Robert continued the interrogation.

"No, nothing like that. She was very careful about not stating who brought the shoes to the store. I questioned how unlikely such a pair of shoes would be purchased in a second-hand thrift store."

"I see." Robert allowed his eyes to leave the road and hold her entire face in the mirror. "But there's more, isn't there? Your questions concerning Marge are about more than this one experience, this one dream, yes?"

Bella's head whipped in Brent's direction. Her eyes were burning. Her mind raced. It was becoming more difficult to deny the fact that Brent said something about the shoes.

Without any words being spoken, Brent knew what Bella was accusing him of. He shook his head nervously. He had not uttered a word about the mirror in the dressing room or the wearing of shoes. But Robert was asking all the right questions that made it appear he knew the secret.

For the next several miles, the three sat in silence as Robert navigated the road. Bella tried to determine if Brent was being honest. And Brent could only sit idly, hoping Robert would not ask him any questions and Bella understood the shaking of his head as a sign of complete loyalty.

The car rocked, first forward then backward, as Robert lifted his foot from the accelerator preparing to enter the city limits of a rival community. The break in the rhythmic flow jarred both passengers and caused them to peer out the front window. Robert took advantage of the change inside the vehicle. "Does Marge have anything to do with this George character?"

"You tell me," Bella responded without looking at the rearview mirror. She spoke to the back of Robert's head.

"I can share with you what I know about George, but I have a feeling that this too has something to do with Marge."

Bella shrugged her shoulders as she said, "I can't say one way or another. I have had other dreams. Dreams about people I have never met, never heard of. These dreams seem to be prompted by Marge."

"Prompted? How so? Does she speak of these people, introduce them to you as it were, and then you dream about them?"

"Yes and no." Bella's body swayed from side to side.

Brent whispered, "Tell him about the shoes."

Without looking in Brent's direction, Bella whispered back, "I can't. He'll think I'm crazy."

Putting his arm around her shoulder, Brent pulled Bella close and asked, "Do you think you're crazy?"

Her head resting against his shoulder, she spoke into his jacket, "I don't know. I meet these people. I see parts of their lives that no one else ever sees. It feels like I am examining their soul."

The news report on George was very preliminary. Robert discovered that George Allen died 10 years prior in Center Pointe, some 500 miles north of the city. He had three daughters and a granddaughter at the time of his death. The daughters are married and live in and around Center Pointe. The granddaughter, Sarah, may be living in the area, but Robert was unable to confirm any recent address.

The news on her dad was even less. In Robert's words, "Every lead hits a brick wall." He promised to keep digging. "Something will shake loose somewhere, I promise."

The remaining nine days of Christmas were less than joyous. Bella was hoping to unwrap gifts that would provide an explanation, if not meaning, to her life.

Chapter 30

Boating and January seldom are two words that appear in the same sentence. Certainly, this was true for those living in the northern third of the states. Yet, both words were heard coming from Bella's soft, high-pitched voice. The conversation responsible for this occurrence was initiated by Marge.

"Bella, did you notice the pristine pair of leather boat shoes that I hung on the wall yesterday?"

"Can't say I did." Looking at the north wall, Bella continued, "Women's or Men's?"

"Men's."

Marge has strategically placed the shoes at eye level next to the opening of the dressing room. It was nearly impossible, while shoving the curtain aside, not to notice the shoes.

"It's January, Marge. I can't imagine many people are thinking about boating, let alone shopping for boat shoes."

"That might be true, but you don't need to own a boat to wear those shoes."

"True, but again, I remind you, it's January! You know our clientele doesn't include many customers who want that type of shoe now. If they were snowmobile boots or five-buckle rubbers, I would understand your excitement."

Still wearing a smile, Marge said, "You're probably right. They just caught my eyes in the back, and I thought what's the difference if they collect dust in the back or out here? They'll be gone before spring arrives, I assure you."

Marge strolled off, leaving Bella to return to the task of picking up items of clothing from under the clothes racks and locating a bare hanger. The basic task afforded Bella time to question what Marge's intentions were. Threading each garment onto the plastic hanger, Bella pondered the significant of the boat shoes that would cause Marge to stop and direct her attention to them. The answer to her question was no mystery to locate, unlike finding a bare hanger to hold the last piece of clothing.

* * *

The relentless onslaught of waves hammered the yacht, tossing the vessel like a ping-pong ball trapped in an air machine. First up and then down, up and down, up and down. To add to the chaos, despite the eight bells ringing announcing four o'clock, the thick density of dark clouds and the cloud bursts resulting in torrential downpours combined to make it as dark as the witching hour. The bow of the yacht was not visible. Panic was the best word to describe what oozed from the pores.

The early season storm caught the couple, a pair of novice sailors at best, totally unprepared to navigate the conditions. The captain of the yacht was Gordon Baker III, a banker, landowner, entrepreneur, and all-around great gentleman. Unfortunately, at that moment, sailing was not among his attributes. Gordon was accompanied by his wife, Shirley Baker. Shirley was thirty years Gordon's junior and equally naïve about sailing.

Possessing a yacht had been Shirley's idea or, better stated, wish, and eventually a demand. A demand stated as, "I want a yacht." Gordon, out of love for his new bride, took up the task of researching and determining that a 1996 Legacy 40 ft yacht directly from the factory would meet their needs and provide Shirley the level of luxury she expected. The interior was finished with cherry woodwork.

Gordon eventually realized that Shirley could not have cared less if the yacht ever left the marina. The craft was meant to serve two purposes, host small social gatherings for influential people and provide a place to sunbathe.

The yacht was still several miles from the mouth of the harbor, and there was no break in the conditions threatening to capsize the vessel. Fearing that survival was not a probable outcome, Shirley could be heard screaming at her husband volumes above the storm. It was an endless string of cursing with an occasional reference to such words as boat, die, hate, and idiot.

Little Lady was tossed into the harbor entrance like an Asian beetle being flicked across the room with a snap of a finger.

When Gordon purchased the yacht in the spring of 1997, at the age of sixty, he christened the vessel in honor of the love of his life. He was well aware of what people said behind his back. How Shirley was a gold digger, an immature twenty-nine-year-old in need of a daddy figure. But she made him happy. He felt young again, and the sex… well, one didn't need to say more.

Bella witnessed the storm and Gordon's tireless efforts to maneuver *Little Lady* to safety in the spring of 2000. She observed an understanding on Gordon's face not previously visible. Bella's hatred of Shirley intensified, recognizing that the blonde bombshell was precisely that, a shell of a person. She was a gold digger who didn't love Gordon but, like a bark beetle, attached herself to a money tree.

After the April storm of 2000, *Little Lady* never left the harbor under the direction of Gordon. Instead, Gordon used the yacht as a place of refuge, a place to center himself. Shirley, on the other hand, used the vessel to entertain charming, ruggedly handsome, up-and-coming businessmen in the early afternoons, leaving herself plenty of sunlight to keep her golden tan glowing. The only time the couple was together on the yacht was Saturday evenings when Shirley hosted small social gatherings.

Gordon welcomed the Saturday evening outings because he would fire up the 420-horse Cat Diesel and pilot the evening cruise about the marina. The gatherings provided the perfect ruse. Gordon could pilot the craft, functioning as a captain, without needing to make any life-saving decisions. And Shirley could buzz about as the queen bee who flashed her jewelry before the other women while flirting with the men getting drunk.

For another seven years, the marriage endured the relentless onslaught of waves hammering the union. Both Gordon and Shirley were worn out from pretending. Pretending that there was something between them. Something worth saving. Something in their vows that had meaning and purpose.

Bella felt relief when she saw in the mirror a suitcase next to the front door of the three-story mansion the couple called home. It felt like she was in a movie theater as she watched and cheered for Gordon when Shirley entered the study to announce her departure. Shirley came around the side of the oak desk to offer Gordon a farewell kiss, a kiss that he refused with a simple turn of his head. "Goodbye, Shirley" was all he said.

Shirley manufactured a few tears that silently rolled down her cheek, leaving a trail of mascara. Gordon raised his hand and repeated the words. "Goodbye, Shirley."

Bella so wanted to reach out herself and kiss Gordon, but elation, the feeling of victory and triumph, was short-lived.

Bella watched as Shirley walked down the sidewalk where she was greeted by a man in a dark suit. The gentleman quickly turned and offered Shirley his arm as he picked up her suitcase with the other hand. Shirley threaded her arm through the small opening and the two pressed against one another and became one. The two figures, now one, continued down the driveway.

An imaginary knife pierced Bella's belly as she scrutinized the stride of the male escorting Shirley. She only saw him from the back, but she knew that stride. She knew it because she had walked beside it. She felt the arm offered to Shirley as the arm offered to protect her. She never saw his face, but she knew his face. She had seen that face nearly every day for the first five years of her life. She was watching her father walk away. Walk away with Shirley. Even more painful, he was walking away from her.

She wanted to scream, to shout at him "STOP!" But her mouth was like a dried-up river bed in the middle of summer. Her face washed with salty tears she took a breath and laughed at herself. What she just witnessed while wearing Gordon's leather deck shoes occurred thirteen years earlier. The truth was, no matter what she told herself in that moment, it hurt to know that her father left her mother and her because he left with Shirley.

Back in the study, Gordon sat quietly. He appeared lighter, as though an anchor had been untied from his neck. An anchor that held his life in check and threatened to drown him.

Bella wondered what if Gordon had not said goodbye. If he had kissed her, would her father be missing? She closed her eyes to consider such a possibility. When she opened her eyes, she saw Gordon as a much older man. A man for whom old age had been cruel. Steadying himself with a cane, he stood next to *Little Lady*. In his free hand was a check for a quarter of a million dollars. His voice was coarse and at times threatened to disappear as he addressed the yacht.

"It took twelve years, but I am finally ready to say goodbye and mean it. Goodbye, *Little Lady*, goodbye."

Gordon lowered his head, and he slowly closed his eyes. At that moment, Gordon vanished, and the mirror was dark.

Chapter 31

Her fingers flew across the face of the phone. She didn't need the assistance of her eyes to locate the appropriate letters. Standing outside the Rerun Thrift Store, filling her lungs with the cold night air, she sent the following text.

"U will never believe what I just discovered about my dad and how I discovered it. This new info, I am sure of it, will help Robert. When can we meet?"

Brent's icon flashed a second after she hit send. He was up and reading the text. She couldn't wait for his response.

"Brent's sort of occupied at the moment, he'll get back to you later."

Her chest tightened. She felt flush. She read the text three times before responding.

"Very funny. Where are u?"

The words that appeared were more disturbing than the first. "Sorry, sister. Your bro is in no condition to read or write. Chad."

Chad? Bella knew immediately what was going on. Brent's so-called buddies, his wrestling teammates, were someplace drinking. He had promised her that he would not hang with those guys. What changed?

"Chad, where are U? I'll come get him."

Nothing. She stared at the phone cradled in her hand as though she could make it vibrate with a return message. She realized that any attempt to rescue Brent was foolish on her part since she didn't have a car. Walking in the direction of home, she contemplated her options should a return text identify the location. None were pleasing.

The nerve endings of her fingers felt the second her phone shook and a light illuminated the screen enabling her to read the text.

"Brent said, go home, Bella. Will text tomorrow."

"Chad, pleas, get him hom safly." Bella's hands trembled as she frantically attempted to respond.

She crawled beneath the hand-stitched quilt, a quilt her grandmother made, praying that Brent would arrive home safely. Her anger was silenced by her fear that something tragic could happen before night's end. Buried beneath the quilt were also the events from earlier in the evening. Although she didn't or couldn't name it, she felt like a yacht being hammered by an endless series of waves. Waves threatening to capsize her life.

The text never arrived. Instead, Brent arrived at Bella's front door.

Seeing that he was safe and only suffering from the lingering effects of dehydration and alcohol poisoning she breathed a sigh of relief followed by anger that flooded her body. She felt the intense burning originating from the inside and moving to the surface of her skin. Literally from the tips of her toes to the crown of her head itched with fury. She wanted to lash out, to strike him, to permit every vulgar word she could imagine to be launched like spitwads against a blackboard.

That's what she wanted, a physical release, a tirade. Something to purge and eradicate the feelings and thoughts that took control of her. That, however, was not what Brent received. What came forth was even worse, worse because it was not expected.

Bella stepped back, giving space for the words she was about to deliver time to hang in the air while being received. Like the sudden burning odor of skunk spray, her words were meant to grow with intensity as they were absorbed.

"Is this what I can expect?" She paused to allow the first wave to penetrate and then continued. "…that every time I need you, you will be nowhere to be found?" Again, she stopped. With a deep breath, she pressed on. "You will be off satisfying some earthly pleasure?"

Brent opened his mouth to reply but was rebuked by Bella's raised hand.

With the same calm, professional manner she delivered her concluding comments as she had the opening. "You better think very carefully before you answer. I don't want to hear any apology, any excuses. Nor do I wish to hear, 'I'm sorry.' The more I think about it, I don't think I want to hear a single word from you at this moment. It's best if you leave."

If Brent had been a turtle, he could have pulled his head into his shell and sought solace, but the best he could do was drop his head to his chest and keep his eyes focused on the carpet. Brent didn't object. He didn't try to defend himself. He simply made his way toward the door. Reaching for the doorknob he heard, "Have Robert contact me. I think I have something that may help him locate my father."

Brent desperately wanted to respond. He wanted to hear what the possible evidence might be. He wanted to lift her and twirl about the kitchen… but… he nodded and continued his departure.

She could not believe the force with which she spoke. She could not believe that she did not completely fall apart in his presence. She could not believe that she could trust herself to do the right thing. The right thing? She would *not* allow herself to become a victim. A victim who condones such behavior. She would *not* allow herself to make excuses for his behavior. She would *not* allow herself to idly stand by and hope, hope he would change. Their future was dependent upon him not letting his addictive behavior guide him. Her love for him enabled her to make difficult choices, choices that might mean she moved forward without him or moved forward with him in a healthy state of mind. If she learned anything from stepping into the shoes of others, it was that she could not live another's life. She could only live her own life.

Chapter 32

It was less than a week until Valentine's Day and Bella didn't have any plans. Marge had not scheduled her to work assuming she and Brent would have plans. Bella's offer to come in and close for anyone who wished to leave early literally stopped Marge as she strolled through the store.

"Say again?"

"I can work on the fourteenth if anyone would like to leave early."

"I scheduled myself to close. I… I assumed everyone would like to get out of here as early as possible, and I don't really have anything… planned."

"I don't either. And I could use the money. Get this, I opened a savings account."

"Girl, you feeling okay? Savings?"

"College!"

"I assumed," Marge paused and looked directly at Bella. "It's none of my business."

"Yeah, well, I haven't said anything. It's been a couple of weeks and well… I don't see any change."

"Sorry."

"Thanks, but there is nothing to be sorry about. It's life, right?"

"It's not quite that simple."

"I know. It's just easier if you know how to pretend it is."

"Fair enough. The fourteenth, you close."

Bella turned to walk away and whispered "thanks" over her shoulder. It was part of the pretending.

Heart-shaped cookies with pink frosting were fanned out on trays throughout the store. Chocolate candy kisses were placed in the store as though they were part of an unannounced scavenger hunt. A 42-inch flat-screen TV attached to a DVD player played the same three movies the entire day, *When Harry Met Sally*, *You've Got Mail*, *Sleepless in Seattle*. By the end of the day, workers were reciting the dialog. Some joked that this wasn't Valentine's Day but Meg Ryan Day.

Bella never questioned what the connection was between Marge and Meg Ryan, but she would not have been surprised to learn that when Marge first arrived in the States, she learned English watching movies. Movies featuring Meg Ryan. Bella also did not want to focus on the fairy tale endings. It was too close, too raw, best to just leave it alone.

Marge, however, had different plans. With the business day drawing to a close and only a handful of customers waiting to use the bathroom before returning to the outdoors to find a place to sleep, Marge called from across the room, "What do you think, Hanks and Ryan equal to the likes of Bogart and Bacall, or Tracy and Hepburn?"

Bella knew the names and had seen a movie or two highlighting the couples of which Marge spoke. She really did not have the energy or the desire to analyze the movies or get pulled into any discussion about Valentine's Day. She simply wanted to get started cleaning up and hoped that by the time she was ready to scrub the floors, the bathroom was no longer occupied and had had time to air out. She tried not to be rude, but her reply was a bit curt.

"I'm not a movie critic. I'm sure if you are really curious, you could find a thorough discussion of the topic online."

Marge never flinched. "I'm sure I could. But I am interested in what you think."

"Honestly," Bella locked eyes with Marge as she replied. "I don't put much thought into such things. I simply watch the movie to be entertained. Movies like these are mindless wanderings."

"Mindless wanderings. That is an intriguing notion." Marge worked in the aisle at the back edge of the store. It was anything but a direct path Bella.

Bella monitored her employer's progression while processing the objective concealed within her statement. *Okay, where is she going with this? I was merely trying to downplay the value of such films. She's doing it again. She's pulling me in, preparing me for something. Be alert. Don't fall for it. Don't be seduced by her tantalizing ways.*

Marge began again. "Mindless wanderings. Are we ever mindless? Is that even possible?"

Bella refused to respond, even though her insiders were screaming with a rebuttal. She wanted to flip the roles and question Marge. *Is it really necessary to analyze everything, every single word?* Instead, she went back to cleaning.

Marge reached the corner, turned right, and proceeded along the north wall next to the shoes. Passing the entrance to the dressing room, she stopped and took up her position. "Even now as you are doing what some may define as mindless work, I bet your mind is working. It is focused. You are thinking, questioning, and framing words and sentences that continue the internal discourse. It's like…" Marge stopped and scanned the room. "It's like…" She turned and looked at the wall of shoes behind her. "It's sort of like… like… this pair of nurse's shoes."

As she raised her arm and pointed at the lone pair of nurse's shoes, Bella's mind worked her internal discourse, *There it is. Those shoes are the objective of this entire conversation.*

Marge continued as she looked at the shoes, "The shoes have a task to perform. If they perform their task and their purpose well, the nurse is not aware of their presence or their work, except for the moment of putting them on and taking them off. Consider everything those shoes have witnessed, both seen and heard. I highly doubt the person to whom the shoes belonged would describe them as worthless simply because they did not acknowledge the shoes' presence every moment."

Bella broke free of the internal discourse that was pondering the uniqueness of the nurse's shoes and mumbled a response. "I get your point. I should have stated more clearly my thoughts concerning such movies. I don't care for that type of movie and for that reason refer to them as mindless."

With a nod, Marge accepted Bella's response and said, "Not everyone wants to be a nurse, and therefore they will never wear a pair of nurse's shoes." She stared at the shoes for another moment and then added, "Lock up after you finish."

Bella uttered, "As always," but Marge was already in her office collecting her coat.

The conversation within her mind resumed. *Why? What's up with that pair of shoes? She was correct, it's a pair I would never have taken down and tried on, but now… now… I need to know.* As she wrestled to understand what she would do the moment the bathroom was clean, she thought about Brent.

She paused before she scrolled through her list of contacts on her phone. She had not had any contact with Brent for several weeks and now she was about to text him. She knew she had to because she promised to inform him whenever trying on a used pair of shoes. The message box was blank as she tried to determine just the right message to send. She had already struck the backspace arrow countless times, erasing several attempts, and then typed, "She did it again. Putting on nurse's shoes."

"WAIT!" Brent texted back.

Bella could see that he was typing more and didn't respond.

His next message read, "B there in 5. Love ya."

Bella's heart skipped a beat as she read the final words of Brent's text. "Love ya." She read them again, and she wanted to cry. Her intent was not to text him to resolve their situation. She reached out because she respected him, she promised him, she… she… damn it, she loved him!

Chapter 33

Carrying a single red rose, Bella stepped into the dressing room. She tried to explain why she hadn't purchased a Valentine's Day gift for Brent, but he refused to listen. Her ears still rang with the words, "Your gift was inviting me to be a part of your life."

Handing her the nurse's shoes, he inquired, "So, what's up with the nurse's shoes?"

"It's hard to explain, but there is no doubt that Marge was directing me to these shoes. There has to be something special."

After a brief pause, she continued, "Since it's Valentine's Day, maybe it's a love story. You know, a nurse meets a sick patient. She helps him recover, and they fall in love and live happily ever after. Or maybe the nurse works in the ER and on Valentine's Day, her lover suffers a tragic accident, arrives in the ER, and the nurse, due to short staffing, must attend to her lover who dies as she tries to save him." Bella was being earnest, not sarcastic.

"Aren't we the happy storyteller?" Brent was expressing his true feelings, He didn't see any correlation between her second scenario and Valentine's Day.

"It's consistent with most of the people I have met and the shoes I have put on. Plus, that's life, isn't it?"

* * *

Blood was everywhere. The patient transported from the ambulance gurney to the ER bed was in shock. He drifted in and out of consciousness.

In a matter of seconds, the space behind the curtain was teaming with staff members. All were skilled at their specific tasks and executed their duties without encumbering one another. The immediate task, as described by the ER doctor, was to stabilize the patient and then determine the severity of his injuries.

As clothing was cut away to determine the source of blood, numerous locations were identified. Each demanded to be cleaned and stitched. However, one gaping puncture wound drew the attention of all eyes in the tiny space. The size and location of the hole dictated the highest priority. With each beat of the heart muscle, blood gushed outward causing the three-inch square flap of skin to rise from the body like a plastic bag caught over an air vent in the city sidewalk. The chasm-like hole on the left side of the body, inches below the heart, was packed off to slow the bleeding. X-rays were considered but it was determined the only hope of saving the patient was to get him into surgery and address the internal damage.

As the bed was wheeled down a long hallway, carrying with it an array of medical supplies to continue feeding the body antibiotics, it passed several doors with windows. It was at one such window that Bella saw the reflection of the nurse who navigated the bed down the hallway. Bella startled and pulled back as though she witnessed a ghost. The face reflected in the glass bore her same features.

That didn't make sense. She wasn't a nurse. She'd never worked in a hospital. The thought of blood made her nauseous. The moment she realized who the woman was in the reflection, the reflection faded as the bed rolled passed.

She vaguely remembered hearing stories of the time her mom worked in the ER at General Hospital. She had just completed nurse's training and had passed the state boards. She needed a job, and that one paid well. The hours were long, there was never a dull moment, the education was beyond description, and the stress... well, the stress was just part of the job.

The bed arrived at the entrance marked surgery, and Bella had not had time to fully grasp that her feet were in her mom's nursing shoes. Twice while en route to the ER the patient's condition demanded immediate attention. The first time, his blood pressure dropped drastically and the second time, he stopped breathing. The rush of the moment consumed Bella as she was pulled deeper into watching the patient struggle to cling to life while the nurse, her mom, worked frantically to save him.

The patient was placed safely in the hands of the surgical team; the heavy metal door swung shut, which acted as a buffer of sorts. The nurse, Bella's mom, who had been at the side of the patient from the moment he passed through the ER doors, leaned against the wall, closed her eyes, and inhaled deeply.

Bella desperately wanted to kick the shoes off. Yet she was unable to place the toe of one shoe against the heel of the other and push. She had to know what happened. She could feel her mom's sense of duty, but... there was something more. Something she, Bella, couldn't identify, couldn't name. Perhaps it was something her mom had not identified herself. Either way, Bella knew she couldn't leave the confines of the dressing room until she understood.

When she allowed herself to look in the mirror, the body of the patient had tubes sprouting from every part of his body. Some of the tubes transported liquid and oxygen into the body while others siphoned liquid from the body. For the moment it was clear the man survived surgery. However, the lack of movement from the patient caused Bella to wonder if his future was still in question.

The breathing tube shoved down the patient's throat obstructed

Bella's vision. She was only able to see the right side of his face and even that wasn't much help as his right eye was nearly swollen shut. Bella swore out loud. "Shit. Shit!" She realized that like the staff who huddled about the body when it arrived in the ER, she never looked at his face. She too was drawn to the blood and the holes covering his torso. "Shit."

Next to the elevated bed which inclined his head slightly stood her mom. She appeared to be evaluating his vitals and checking the bandages for any excess bleeding. However, the moment she stepped back and absorbed the data sprinting across the screen on the monitor, Bella observed that her mom's right hand cradled the patient's left hand. Bella squinted in hopes of judging the meaning of the connection, but at that moment the scene in the mirror went blank. Bella was left staring at her own reflection and bottom of the nurse's shoes.

Untying the shoes and removing her feet, she wanted to throw the shoes at the mirror. She was certain there was more to discover about her mom and the patient. But a degree of wisdom stopped her arm from moving forward for she knew the laws of physics and the likelihood of breaking the mirror. Something she couldn't risk.

Exiting the dressing room, she stared directly into Brent's face, which was filled with anticipation like a child eager to tear into the gifts beneath the Christmas tree. His voice confirmed that he was overcome with hunger to hear what Bella experienced.

"Well, what did you see? Was it a love story?"

"The mirror went blank? Blank as in..."

"Blank! Nothingness. Dark. Blank!" Bella couldn't hide her frustration. Not even from Brent who was just trying to be supportive.

Driven back by her words, the excitement written on his face sagged into bewilderment.

Acknowledging the confusion displayed before her, Bella realized that it wasn't Brent's fault. With her best compassionate tone, she said, "I'm sorry. This isn't your fault. I don't know what happened. I don't get it. One minute I was watching my mom hold this guy's hand and..."

"Your mom?" Pointing at the shoes in Bella's hand, he asked, "Those shoes were, are, your mom's?"

"Yeah. From when she was right out of college working at an intercity ER. Some guy was brought in with massive cuts and punctures to his upper body, and she was one of the nurses working to save his life. But I felt something more. It was more than sympathy. It felt... it felt like... oh, I don't know. I was so close to..." Bella could not finish the thought because she had no idea what the thought was.

The two of them stood in silence staring at the shoes as though the shoes would speak the answer.

Brent reached out and pulled Bella into his body. His arms wrapped around her body as he held her tight.

She allowed herself to become a ragdoll. She knew he would hold her. Despite what transpired previously, she knew she could trust him.

Without releasing her, Brent suggested that perhaps she was trying too hard.

Leaning back just enough to look directly into his eyes, she asked, "What do mean, trying too hard?"

Brent spoke slowly to ensure that each word delivered was precisely what he meant. "Obviously, I have not experienced any of this firsthand, but from what you have told me, it seems like with all the other experiences, you let it unfold. And with this one, well... maybe... you were too invested."

"Invested?" With both hands she shoved him back, giving herself space. "Invested? Of course, I'm invested. This is my mom, and I think she is feeling something for this guy. And I have no idea who he is or why his body has been ripped to shreds."

Attempting to close the gap between them, he took a step forward and waited for her reaction before speaking. When she stood still, he offered up, "That's my point. You are too close to this story. You're trying to make it happen on your time and not your mom's. The mirror doesn't have a concept of time, does it?"

She didn't need to respond. There was no concept, no notion of time when she entered the dressing room. Instead, she closed her eyes and thought about the first time she wore the stiletto heels.

His question brought her back, "Bella, what are you thinking?"

With a single nod, she said, "You might be right. No, you *are* right. I need to try it again and be patient. I need to let the story, whatever it is, unfold on its own."

Before she returned to the dressing room with the nursing shoes in hand, she gave Brent a long lingering kiss and said, "That should hold you until I return." As an afterthought, she added, "No matter how long it takes."

Bella knew her strengths and weaknesses well. Her AP Psychology class offered a host of different assessments to measure and identify a person's attributes. Unfortunately, knowing these was one thing. Being able to employ the strengths at the appropriate moment and develop strategies to grow was quite another. For the essay question on the unit test, she described in detail how knowing the qualities of Responsibility, Loyalty, Team Player, Reasonable, and Trustworthy aided in the development of her emotional intelligence and self-awareness. Acknowledging these areas of strength coupled with an awareness of areas of weakness enabled her to have a great appreciation of diversity. She concluded the three-page essay by identifying how she planned to become a more patient person. Impatience was scored as her greatest weakness. Proof-reading the essay, she considered adding the words, Blah, Blah, Blah, to the end, but since honesty wasn't among her top five attributes, she decided it wasn't necessary. Besides, she was sure the teacher would take offense and lower her grade.

Staring at the blank mirror confirmed that no amount of effort, no strategic plan, no baa, baa, baa was going to make her a more patient person. Her fingernails chewed down as far as possible, Bella acknowledged that her impatience was compounded by the fact that it was her mom who apparently controlled the situation. She wasn't sure of the source of the irritation but when it came to her mom, she had zero patience. It escalated when a friend commented on how cool her mom was. It annoyed her how well Brent and her mom got along with each other. Even worse was whenever Brent questioned her rude behavior directed toward her mom. Her response was "You don't live with her. You have no idea."

Seated in relative darkness, waiting for the mirror to come to life, Bella gave space to a sliver of vulnerability. Perhaps what Brent didn't understand, couldn't understand was the presence of a third party who wasn't present. Bella pondered the possibility that she unconsciously blamed her mom for the absence of her father. She wondered why there was a dense fog that hid and muted any conversation concerning his disappearance. Her internal voice trembled as she asked, *Does Mom know what happened to him, or where he might be at this moment? Either above or within the earth? And if so, why? Why was she keeping it from her?*

Her inability to resolve this quandary was slowly consuming her. If she was honest with herself, she had to confess that her lack of patience with her mom was only part of the story. Truth be told, she was more impatient with herself for not pressing the issue, for not demanding answers, for not solving the riddle. *If only...* she stopped herself. She couldn't give voice to the thought. *If only... there was a pair... NO, DON'T THINK IT!*

Chapter 34

Her index finger pressed the aglet, the plastic end of the shoelace, into her thumb to the point that it left an indentation. It wasn't until she recognized that squeezing the plastic end of the shoelace was a feeble attempt to manipulate the mirror that she relaxed her index finger, and the aglet dropped free and struck the side of the nurse's shoe. To combat her impatience, she closed her eyes and took several deep breaths.

From behind her eyelids, she saw the presence of light. The mirror was alive. She turned her head slightly to the left so that her right ear might absorb any sound. She determined it was more important to hear, to listen, than to see. Using the sound, the noises that spilled from the mirror, her mind would create a picture of what was happening.

She heard and her body felt the rush of air propelled by a fan that brought goosebumps to her arms. There was another rush of air that yielded a hissing sound as though pushed through a tiny tube. A high-pitched squeak sporadically dominated the airwaves like Michael Jordan's high tops striking a waxed basketball floor. Muffled tones, as though spoken into a pillow, sputtered along. The actual words were beyond discernment, but... Bella searched the recesses of her mind.

The voices sounded familiar, and yet not. Her head rolled to the right to enable her left ear to offer discernment. Based on the last scene viewed in the mirror, she determined the voices belonged to her mom and maybe the doctor or another hospital staff member. She leaned forward to narrow the distance that the vibrations traveled in the hope of clarifying to whom the voices belonged. Familiar and yet not quite.

Beneath all these sounds was the consistent click of the second hand from a clock as it labored to give balance to the space and to mark the moment in time, in history. The rhythm, the uninterrupted rhythm, offered Bella an interlude of peace. She no longer felt the need to press the scene but to allow it to wash over her and through her. The clicks grew louder. They muted every other sound. She understood it was time to open her eyes.

Her eyelids fluttered open. The brightness momentarily blinded her. She pulled back and squinted. Her eyes adjusted like a camera lens, and the scene before her came into focus. There was her mom, seated in a chair next to the man in the bed. The man... the man...

Like an avalanche racing down the face of a mountain consuming everything in its wake, Bella's eyelid clamped tight. The man!

"My god, the man!" The words overwhelmed every inch of her brain.

Chapter 35

"You can tell your brother he doesn't need to continue searching for my dad." Those were the first words Bella spoke after kicking her mom's nursing shoes from her feet while pressing her back against Brent's chest.

"You know where he is?" Brent could hardly control his curiosity. The words just escaped from his mouth like a wild mustang smelling freedom.

He initially didn't know what to think or how to respond as Bella emerged from the dressing room. For several minutes, she didn't say a word. She just stared off into space. When he was about to rise from the floor, she waved at him to stay put and then proceeded to walk over to him and lower herself into his lap.

She heard Brent's question, but she didn't have the energy at that moment to respond. Resting against his body, feeling his presence, and hearing the rhythm of his breathing created a sense of safety. Safe like a fetus in a mother's womb. In her mother's womb? Mom? What mom? Whose womb?

Trying to imagine what Bella might have witnessed that would traumatize her to such a degree, Brent finally broke the silence. "Can you tell me what you saw?"

With her head slowly rocking from side to side, Bella spoke. "I saw the entire chronology of my parents' relationship. I saw their first kiss…"

Brent interrupted the account. "That can't be that awful."

"Their first kiss was between two infatuated twenty-something people. Remember our first kiss? Not that different." Brent wore a smile as she spoke. "You want to watch your parents kissing knowing that the kiss is merely a prelude to more?"

Shaking his head, no longer smiling, Brent said, "Yeah, no."

Bella continued, "I saw my dad get down on one knee and propose. There was their wedding with all the day and night events, the purchasing and moving into our home. I witnessed it all, the good times and the bad. But none of that compared to where their story started." Bella took several deep breaths before she was able to continue.

"The man, the man who came through the ER doors, the man whose body resembled a pin cushion, the man my mom took care of would eventually become her husband, my dad. Or the person I call Dad."

"The person you call Dad? I don't understand."

Bella leaned forward to turn and face Brent as she spoke. "You will. I got ahead of myself. I'll give you the entire story."

The weight of the details that started as a love story and quickly expanded to include unimaginable events fit for a Jodi Picoult novel or a Greg Iles suspense story made it difficult for Brent to keep his jaw from striking his chest.

The reason Brent's brother could not locate Bella's dad was because he didn't exist. He didn't exist because he belonged to a secret agency that had infiltrated the mob. Unfortunately for her dad, his cover was exposed when he rescued the wife of a mob killer, Mrs. Shirley Baker. A woman, from a professional standpoint, he should not have rescued and thereby maintained his position in the mob. To protect Bella and her mom, he had to cut all ties with them. For her own wellbeing, her mom couldn't risk telling her the truth. Silence seemed like the best option, the only option.

"Brent, you need to tell your brother to stop immediately. Any attempts to find my dad are dangerous. I am putting him at risk, assuming..." Bella stopped herself. Thinking it was one thing; giving it a voice was quite another. She had no choice. She had to say it. "Assuming he is still alive."

"I'm speechless. I... I don't know what to say."

"There's more."

"More? What else could there be?"

With a puff of air, Bella continued, "I saw myself being placed for the first time in the arms of my mom and then passed to my dad." After shaking her head, she said, "I wasn't a newborn. We were not in the hospital."

The words spilled out before he could stop himself. "Wait, what? You're... you're... adopted?"

"Yeah. Supposedly when my dad was on some secret mission overseas, he was exposed to radiation that made him sterile."

"How old were you when... well, you know... when you were adopted?"

"I was a couple of months old. My bio mom tried to keep me but discovered as a teen mom she wasn't prepared. My parents fostered me and then did the paperwork to legally adopt me."

Brent carefully chose his words as he asked, "So did you see your mom? I mean, your bio mom?"

Wiping a single tear from her eye, Bella said, "No, some social worker delivered me. But I have this feeling that I have seen her."

"Seen her?" Brent shook his head. "I don't understand."

"I don't totally understand either. It's just a... feeling. I feel like I have seen my bio mom somewhere."

The two sat in silence for several minutes before Brent asked, "Not that this isn't enough, but was there anything else?

Bella smiled and surveyed the entire store before she answered. "It may be insignificant, considering everything else I learned this evening, but…" She paused for another moment to scan the inside of the Rerun Thrift Store a second time. "Turns out my mom got me this job?"

"Your mom? How?" Brent couldn't believe what he had just heard. There was no indication that Bella's mom and Marge knew one another.

"I know. Who would have figured that Mom and Marge not only know one another but are friends? I can't remember Mom asking about Marge or Marge referencing my mom. But right there, live before my very eyes in the mirror, was Mom out to lunch with Marge and asking if she might have something at the store I could do. She told Marge I needed to learn how to take responsibility and get my ass out of bed."

"Now that sounds like your mom. At least about taking responsibility."

Without cracking a smile, Bella responded, "No, it's the 'ass out of bed' that sounds like my mom. She just doesn't swear around you."

Extending his arm, Brent placed his hand on Bella's thigh and slowly massaged her leg as he said, "Bella. I don't know what to say. What are you thinking, feeling?"

Rubbing his cheek with the tip of her fingers she said, "Honestly? Other than numbness, I don't feel anything. I can't let myself feel because it would be too overwhelming." Pulling back slightly and looking directly into his eyes she continued. "What I need right now is for you to hold me."

It was the first night since Marge opened the Rerun Thrift Store that the bathroom wasn't scrubbed.

Chapter 36

"Bella, phone." Bella's mom called from the living room. "Bella! Get up and come to the phone. It's work. Something about the bathroom."

Tossing the covers aside and rubbing the sleep from her eyes, Bella swore under her breath. By the time she reached the living room, she was able to speak in a civil tongue. "I'm so sorry, Marge. I'll be right down and take care of the bathroom. What's that? No, nothing happened. Brent just arrived early to give me a ride home, and I totally forgot the bathroom. The light? I thought I turned it off, but I might have forgotten."

Bella's mom stepped from the kitchen into the living room and asked, "Is everything okay?"

"Yeah. Work was a bit stressful last night, and when Brent arrived early, I just forgot about cleaning the bathroom." She surprised herself as she spoke. Normally she would have questioned why it was any business of her mom. The need to become defensive and poke at her mom seemed to have evaporated. She had an overwhelming desire to hug the woman who stood before her with a dish towel in hand, whose sweatpants and hooded sweatshirt were two sizes too large, meant to hide the effects of gravity. Instead, she elected to change the direction of the conversation as she returned the phone to its cradle.

"Mom, we must be the only people on the face of the planet who still have a landline. Why don't you get rid of this phone? You have a cell phone. I mean, who actually uses this number anymore to call us?" The moment she finished the question she knew the answer, Marge and...

"I suppose I could disconnect that phone, but... I'm not sure everyone has my cell phone number. I wouldn't want to miss an important call."

Bella understood completely. She also understood that this wasn't the moment to make her mom announce from whom that important call might originate. "I suppose you're right. I better shower and get down to the store to clean up the bathroom."

* * *

Bella had hoped that the additional five hours since the bathroom was last used, would provide plenty of time for the smell to dissipate. Unfortunately, the interim period only compounded the odor. The smell burned the inside of her nose as soon as she stepped through the doorway.

"You might want a gas mask," Marge shouted from the office.

"Do we have one?"

"No. But you might want one."

Narrowing the distance from the front door to the bathroom, Bella had to inquire,

"How is it possible that it got worse? It didn't smell like this last night. If it had, I never would have forgotten."

"Was Harry the last person in the store last evening?"

"Let me think." Bella stood still and stared off as she replayed the arrival and exit of

people in the store. "Yeah, I think he was. Now that I think about it, Brent almost ran into him when he arrived." After another brief pause, she continued, "At the time, I didn't give it much thought, but Harry didn't appear to be himself last night. Normally he stops to say hello, but he didn't say a word to me. The Thinker was off his game."

"That might explain why he ignored the signs reminding him to flush."

"Oh, don't tell me! Please, don't tell me!" Bella realized what awaited her in the toilet.

An hour and a half later the Rerun Thrift Store no longer smelled like a backed-up sewer.

Bella prepared to return home for a lazy Saturday of doing nothing as she held the door open for Elmer, a sporadic visitor to the store, who stumbled through the doorway. The serious look chiseled on Elmer's face resulted in a sudden change of plans. Bella decided she could postpone the lure of nothingness for a few minutes to hear what made Elmer appear so exasperated.

Elmer was a colorful character whose life story required a box of twenty-four Crayola crayons to thoroughly capture the bright and dark moments of his life and everything in between. Currently, he was living in the shade of yellow-green. Elmer described it as such, yet quickly acknowledged that it felt as though his life was always on the edge of fading. He feared the possibility of waking up to a world that was no longer yellow or green but drifting into the hues of darkness, life as brown or black.

As a real estate broker, Elmer was riding the spaceship of a skyrocketing housing market. Fifteen years on the back side of college, having just celebrated his thirty-seventh birthday, Elmer could say with confidence that he was wealthy. He wasn't just rich; he was wealthy. With the assistance of Matt, his best friend from college who had become a financial planner, Elmer had developed an impressive investment portfolio. Just five years earlier he started his real estate brokerage and hired several real estate agents, including a significant number of support staff. The rumblings of a troubled housing market in the early days of 2007 didn't deter Elmer as Matt assured him, he could ride out any hiccup in the market. On the second of January, 2008, Elmer realized that his spaceship was running out of fuel. The brightness of his life was fading; he described it as tan.

On the sixth day of February, Ash Wednesday no less, the color of Elmer's world became a charcoal, sooty world. His wife, his college sweetheart, his companion in navigating the spaceship, informed him that she was leaving him. The brutality was greater than simply asking for a divorce. At the breakfast table, she informed him that Matt and she had been lovers for years. In fact, going all the way back to college. She had planned to divorce Elmer years earlier, but his financial success made it impossible. Now that he was poor, it wasn't too difficult.

Elmer objected to the idea that he was poor. Enjoying the task way too much, the love of his life delivered the news that Matt had overcalculated his financial stability, and he was wiped out. As if that wasn't enough, she finished breakfast by sharing that there was less than a fifty percent chance that their fourteen-year-old daughter was his. With a smile, she said, "We can do a DNA test. If she's Matt's daughter, you won't have to pay child support."

As his glass of orange juice covered the far wall in the kitchen, Elmer told her, "She's my daughter no matter what some stupid test might reveal. Besides, I'd never put her through that."

Several years after the divorce, Elmer learned that Matt and his ex-wife hid all his money in several offshore accounts.

Unfortunately, the color of Elmer's world continued to fade. The third week in March of that same year, as his daughter was walking home from school, a drunk driver in a pickup jumped the curb and struck her. The paramedics at the scene said that she was dead before she hit the ground. Any light, any color was now absent from his existence. Elmer sunk deep into a depression and within six months was living on the streets.

As winter set in, he moved to the railroad yard. He lived in a world of blackness. Nothing existed. He contemplated night and day stepping in front of a train and putting an end to his misery. He told Bella one night, shortly after she started working at the Rerun Thrift Store, that the only thing that kept him alive was the thought that such an action would have disappointed his daughter if she were alive.

As the months became years of living in the railroad yard, Elmer learned the skills of various jobs associated with the railroad. He became friends with a few of the workers. He asked questions about their jobs and eventually applied for an open position as a rail yard worker. He was hired with a laugh, "Well, you'll never have an excuse for being late." Over time and with compassion from management, he became an engineer.

Eventually, he moved out of the railroad yard and into a one-room apartment above an empty storefront building. Despite not bedding down each night in a cardboard box, he never lost touch with those who called the railroad yard home. Whenever possible he would offer to assist anyone willing to change the color of their world with complete awareness that such a change didn't start with him.

With Bella in tow, Elmer stood in the doorway of Marge's office and said he had sad news to share.

It was then that Bella noticed that Elmer cradled a pair of shoes close to his chest. To an untrained eye, it might appear that Elmer carried an infant. With all the precautions necessary to ensure the shoes were not dropped, Elmer delivered a pair of penny loafers to the top of Marge's desk along with the following report. "Harry died sometime during the night. These were his shoes."

Marge choked out, "Do you know what happened? I don't recall him saying he wasn't feeling well." Looking past Elmer to Bella, she added, "Although Bella did say that he didn't act like himself last night when he came in to use the bathroom."

Stepping to Elmer's side, Bella stared at the shoes on the desk as she described Harry's quiet demeanor. When she finished, she couldn't resist and questioned why the shoes of a homeless man were brought to the store.

Elmer smiled and rubbed his chin before he answered. "This might sound silly, but I made old Harry a promise."

Bella caught a twinkle in Marge's eye as Elmer continued.

Elmer backtracked to provide a context for the promise.

"Well, it was more like I agreed to carry out his final wish. God, it had to be..." Elmer paused. It was as if one could see him going back in time until the precise moment appeared in his mind's eye. "It had to be at least ten years ago. We were polishing off a cheap bottle of whiskey." As an afterthought, he added. "I don't remember how or who came up with the money to make the purchase, but I do remember we passed the fifth back and forth savoring every swallow. It was one of the rare moments in the yard where we allowed ourselves to be vulnerable and share a glimpse into our past."

Elmer looked about the small office space for a place to sit. The only chair in the room, other than the one Marge held down, was buried beneath several boxes held together loosely by string. Rather than attempt to move the boxes he selected an oversized box in the corner that appeared to be more stable. Once seated, he continued.

"Life in the yard has its own rules and social norms. You watch out for one another, and yet you don't trust one another. You have acquaintances. You know who belongs and who doesn't. But you don't track every person's coming and going. You don't make friends, yet survival could be dependent upon having a friend. You don't want to be noticed, yet you're the safest when you are visible. You might say life in the yard is a paradox. There are no rules and yet without rules, no one survives. More challenging, the rules are not written, never spoken, but always enforced."

Elmer leaned into the corner. It was obvious that in the recesses of his mind, he was back living in the yard as one of the homeless. Marge instructed Bella to fetch Elmer a cup of coffee.

"If I remember correctly, two packets of sugar. One before you pour the coffee and one after."

Elmer smiled and said, "Just one. Trying to cut down on my sugar intake. Pre-diabetic."

From outside the office, Bella shouted back, "One it is. Be right back." As promised, Bella returned in less than two minutes carrying three cups of coffee.

Blowing into the Styrofoam cup to cool the contents before taking several sips, Elmer continued. "As challenging as being homeless is, it's the myths surrounding homelessness that make it even more difficult."

Bella's brow wrinkled as she asked, "Myths?"

"Yeah, the myths make it convenient to ignore homeless people or to justify the homelessness. The myths make it easier not to see the person as a human being but as an illness."

Bella interrupted Elmer. "Before I started working here, I assumed homeless people were mentally ill. I never thought there might be other factors. I remember a teacher once saying, 'Some homeless people live on the street because they choose to live that way. At the time, I never thought to question such a statement."

"That's just the tip of the list of myths." Elmer chuckled, not that the words he was about to share were funny. Quite to the contrary. He chuckled because he was sitting in the Rerun Thrift Store nursing a cup of coffee and because of what he was about to share. "Harry, recognizing that I was new to life in the rail yard, mentored me on how to survive. I made the promise to bring his shoes to the store and to deliver them to you, Marge, because Harry was my friend. I never asked why. I never inquired what was so special about that pair of penny loafers. I didn't even say, 'Yes, I would bring the shoes.' I just nodded. Harry knew I would follow his wish." Elmer fell silent.

After a respectful amount of time, Marge lifted her Styrofoam cup and said, "To Harry. He will be missed."

As the three cups were lowered, Marge instructed Bella to take the shoes into the backroom and clean them.

Chapter 37

The leather cleaner, which was saddle soap sold in a yellow round tin, worked its magic. As Bella spread the yellow paste in a circular motion penetrating through years of dirt, grime, and continuous exposure to the natural elements, the fibers of the leather absorbed the paste. The results were the return of luster and suppleness. Witnessing the resurrection of life within each shoe, Bella wondered if beneath the crusty, impenetrable layers of brittle, callused skin, there existed a suppleness and luster within Harry. It took her breath away momentarily when she realized that she would never again inhale the musky, whisky scent that greeted her ahead of Harry's physical appearance. She decided that she would ask Marge to purchase a fifth of cheap whisky and have the staff toast Harry.

The loafers sat amid a small clearing on the table surrounded by a mountain of clothes that needed to be sorted and either folded or placed on a hanger for display. The richness of the shoes became obvious. These were not just any old pair of penny loafers. Retrieving her phone from her pocket, Bella searched for penny loafers. The rabbit hole of searching pulled her deeper until she was reading the origin of the shoe.

The allure was that the origin of the loafer was shrouded in controversy. Two tales existed to explain the possible source for creating such a shoe. Both accounts had varying degrees of credibility. For Bella, however, the latter story was more attractive. The most popular account, at least based on sites detailing the history of penny loafers, described Americans traveling northern Europe at the start of the 20th century who encountered Norwegian fishermen wearing "teasers." The practical design provided comfort and safety while working in wet slippery conditions. The world travelers returned home searching for comparable footwear only to discover none existed. The second account suggests that the loafer didn't originate on foreign soil but among the Native Americans. The moccasin style became the initial design for the loafer. All accounts agreed that the company G.H. Bass sold the first pairs of loafers. In 1936 ads appeared highlighting the "weejun" that featured a decorative strap across the top of the shoe. The shoe quickly became popular among elite, wealthy businessmen, and eventually became the trademark of Ivy League students.

The fad of a penny placed in the loafer emerged at the same time the shoes became a staple on college campuses. With a penny safely tucked in each shoe, so the theory went, one was never without money to place a phone call in case of an emergency. Bella struggled to comprehend how a penny could be used to place a call until she remembered their landline, which brought forth images from old movies and the payphone.

A quick check of the loafers revealed that a penny rode atop each shoe. Bella wondered if this was the doing of Harry or if the pennies came with the shoes. Was he even aware of their existence and if so, were they meant to serve as a lifeline in case of an emergency? At that moment Bella knew the next time she closed, she would carefully slide her feet into shoes. A shiver rippled through her body. The thought of her feet touching the place where Harry's foot last was too much. She wasn't sure there was enough disinfectant to kill whatever might be growing in the creases of the shoes.

Much to Bella's surprise when she carried the loafers to the front of the store, Marge told her to leave the shoes in the back for a few days.

"Maybe a week from now would be a good time to shelf them. Sort of honor Harry's memory by keeping them in the back. I doubt they will be here more than a day once they're shelved. You work Saturday, yes?"

Bella nodded and before she could speak, Marge said, "Good, then you can put them out before you leave work next Saturday night."

Chapter 38

The dilemma for Bella, when her eyes focused and realized it was only Sunday morning, was that Saturday evening could not arrive quickly enough. The interim of 160 hours at best, assuming she could lock the Rerun Thrifty Store door by ten, provided too much... too much time to think, to contemplate what she would encounter as her foot slid into Harry's penny loafers.

With the blanket pulled to her chin and her head pressed deep into the pillow, she fell victim to her internal voice. The voice that viewed everything from a philosophical position. It was this voice that pushed Brent away and welcomed him back. It was this voice that questioned Marge's intentions. The voice was now, again, forcing her to define what exactly occurred when she put on another person's shoes. The voice prodded her to dig beyond the obvious. *How is it you can see and hear the lives of those who owned the footwear?*

She reassured herself that the how didn't matter anymore. The simple fact was she could. The stinging question, the one that gave her inner voice, voice, was, why? Why should she have such a gift? A *gift*!

Bella scoffed at such a notion. A gift? A snort escaped just before she informed her inner voice that it could be debated for hours whether these experiences were indeed gifts.

The voice, as it always did, controlled the ensuing discourse and assured her that the issue at the moment was not about labeling the experience. Whether it was a gift or not did not alter the experience or, at this moment, Bella's desire to journey into Harry's life.

"Ah!" the voice proudly sighed.

"Ah, what?"

"Ah, there's the why! It is about journeying into the lives of people."

Bella's feet kicked violently as the blanket flew to the end of the bed. She tried not to think for a moment. But of course, it's impossible not to think. Thinking about not thinking is thinking. "Damn you!"

"You know precisely why you're frustrated with yourself at this moment."

Slowly Bella acknowledged, "Yes." After several minutes of silence she shared, "God, I hate this."

"And what exactly do you dislike?"

Besides this voice that refused to shut up? "I... I hate to state the truth."

"What about the truth scares you?"

"It strips you naked. It leaves you vulnerable. It..."

"Yes??? It what?"

"God, now I really hate work! This whole experience has been about the soul. Not the shoe, but the soul. The essence of one's existence."

"Your existence, their existence, or maybe... both?"

"Mom!" Bella shouted, "What's for breakfast?"

Bella's mom appeared in the doorway. "Sorry, did you call me?"

With the sheet partially covering her torso, she responded, "I was wondering what's for breakfast."

"You mean, you're getting up already? It's only"—she quickly checked her watch—"ten a.m."

"I can't lay here awake. It's too much."

"Well, how about pancakes?"

"Let me shower, and I'll come help."

Skeptical that she heard her daughter correctly she stumbled over the word, "Okay."

*　*　*

The cheap whiskey tasted as Bella expected, cheap. Not that she knew how fine whiskey tasted, or any whiskey. She toasted Harry's life with the other staff prior to the opening of the store for the day. The idea came from Bella. Marge immediately agreed and added, "I should have thought of it. It is so fitting." Since it was her idea, she asked Marge if she could have a second shot.

The second burned her throat less than the first, and the liquid seemed to slide down easier. Maybe it was the result of feeling warm and lightheaded. She didn't care why.

Marge smiled as she watched Bella sip the contents that everyone else swallowed in one quick tip of the plastic shot glass.

Realizing that she had become the center of attention as her co-workers waited for her to finish the second shot, she felt compelled to say something. "I think the day may just go a bit faster."

In the midst of laughter, Marge surmised, "Perhaps that is why Harry drank cheap whiskey. It made the time pass more quickly."

Weaving slightly from side to side, Bella said, "Maybe." She paused and then added, "But does it really?"

At her office door, Marge stopped and turned back to Bella and said, "I'll check in with you at six this evening and we'll see."

By three o'clock, Bella concluded the whiskey had little effort on the flow of time. If anything, time seemed to move slower. To make matters worse, two overly made-up women, from the north side lingered. Their fingers weighed down by priceless stones appeared to touch every item on the shelves and graze through the garments hanging on the racks. Bella suspected that the high society socialites were convincing themselves that they were in touch with the less fortunate population. She was sure that at the next club gathering of those who have a live-in housekeeper, a nanny to raise the kids, and a husband with a seven-figure income, these two would report how they gained a new appreciation as well as empathy for those who struggle to have a meaningful life. Before the meeting ended and cocktails were served, the two women would appoint themselves as co-chairs to plan and organize the next service project for the purpose of making the community better and safer.

Holding Harry's loafers, Bella recognized that she was as judgmental and hypocritical as the two socialites. With a smile, she acknowledged that her scenario reeked of stereotyping and cheap whiskey. Yet she also admitted that the time spent creating the tale kept her from being rude and asking them to hurry up. Gripping the loafers even tighter she wondered what Harry might have said to the shoppers. Unlike many of the others who wandered in to use the facilities, she could not recall a time Harry ever spoke to customers. He would stop and chat with the workers but not the customers. And of course, the chat was always thought-provoking.

It was at that moment that one of the women, the one whose fingernail polish matched her hairclip and shoes, asked the price of the loafers.

Startled to be acknowledged, Bella stuttered a response. "Yeah, they're not for sale."

"They're yours'?" The woman pressed her.

"Um, no. They..." Bella struggled to choose the correct words. She didn't want to lie, but she couldn't let the shoes leave the store without putting them on. Then she remembered Marge's directive, "*Put them out before you leave.*" Speaking with an edge of authority Bella informed the woman that the shoes would be available next week.

The woman quickly countered, "But we're not going to be here next week. We are here now. Name your price."

"The price is 25.00 dollars..." After a pause, Bella added, "Next week. Anything else you are interested in purchasing?"

"Yes, there are several items..."

An hour and a half later and several hundred dollars added to the till, Bella noticed it was five-thirty. Before long she could report that cheap whiskey didn't impact the measurement of time.

Six o'clock arrived, and Marge had not emerged from her office. The door was shut. Something that seldom occurred. Bella had not noticed when the door closed. In part because a third shot clouded her cerebral cortex and because as the fog lifted the two women demanded her attention.

At seven, Bella asked a fellow employee if she had seen Marge during the afternoon.

"Not since we toasted Harry."

"The office door is closed. I wonder if she left?" Bella's words were more directed toward herself than asking a question of her colleague.

"She must have. She never shuts the door unless someone is getting canned." As an afterthought, the semi-retired former elementary school teacher added, to justify the door remaining open, "Too many boxes to move."

A few minutes after eight o'clock Bella's curiosity took charge. She convinced herself that something had to be wrong. This wasn't like Marge. Even if she departed for the day, she would have announced her departure. There was only one shopper in the store and one rail yard tenant in the bathroom. Now was the time to investigate Marge's office.

Knuckles struck the door softly. Once, twice, she waited. Again, but with slightly more force. Once, twice, and a third time for good measure. Nothing.

The third attempt included aggression against the wooden door and a whisper that accompanied the rapping. "Marge?" Once, twice. Silence. The knob turned effortlessly. The door was not locked. Bella used her voice again, "Marge? You in here?" Nothing.

Her fingers located the light switch and the bright glow drove the darkness back into the corners revealing a body cascading down the chair.

"Marge!" Bella screamed. The body did not move. It would have been easier for Bella to move if the soles of her feet were buried in cement than to confront death. Despite the desire to rush to Marge's side and shake her shoulders to bring life to a lifeless body, Bella could not move.

Moving. It's something that once a person masters, placing one foot in front of the other and maintaining balance, one does not consciously give it additional thought. It just happens until it doesn't and then at that moment sweat pours forth in an effort to move the body that will not or cannot.

Bella's paralysis was not due to injury or a stroke but was initiated by shock. Bella's inner voice knew what awaited her when she touched the body. Her brain was giving her body time, a moment to accept the truth, to ponder the soul that had escaped Marge's body.

* * *

With Brent on her right and her mom on her left, Bella watched in silence as the county coroner pronounced the official end of Marge's life. She told herself she was supposed to cry. She was supposed to demonstrate sorrow. But unlike her mom who sobbed to the point of nearly passing out, and Brent who attempted to hide the streams of salty water washing his cheeks, her face was dry. Sorrow evaded her as her thoughts were directed to the future of the Rerun Thrift Store.

Would the store open on Monday? What would happen to the railroad tenets? And what about Harry's penny loafers? Would she, *could* she slide her feet into those shoes?

Standing contemplating the future, her hand graced the side of her jeans. She felt the outline of the key to the front door. In discussion with her inner voice, she vowed that for the foreseeable future, the store would remain open.

Chapter 39

It was Sunday. In honor of everything Marge taught her, if for no other reason, Bella decided she would slip on the loafers. It may be the last time she'd experience such an event. Of course, there was another reason for placing her feet in the penny loafers. Harry.

Opening the door for Brent, she stared again at the sign she taped to the door.

Temporarily Closed
Due to the Untimely Passing of
A Lovely Woman
Marge

It was her fourth attempt at writing the perfect message. Even though the store was closed on Sunday, she felt the world needed to know that Marge's soul no longer was present in the Rerun Thrift Store, or was it?

Brent commented as he brushed past her, after a quick kiss, "It seems strange to enter the building in daylight. Although, after last night, I'm not sure how I'd feel about coming after dark."

Bella locked the door behind them and said, "I'm not sure what to expect. I've never done this in the daylight. I hope there's nothing magical about the darkness."

The penny loafers sat alone next to the curtain of the dressing room. Bella placed them there the moment she arrived. She wasn't sure why that was demanded of her. She awoke at 3:23 in the morning to a vision of the shoes perfectly placed outside the dressing room. Whatever it was, a directive from her inner voice, from Marge, from Harry himself, it had been delivered. She wasn't about to challenge it.

Next to each other, Bella and Brent stood in the aisle between women's blouses on one side and plus-size pajamas on the other side. Neither spoke as they stared at the shoes, followed by a quick glance into the dressing room. Did the curtain move? Both thought they saw something, but they could not bring themselves to express the absurd. It was impossible. They were the only ones in the building. The events of the past twelve hours were making them nervous.

The curtain did move, but only at the hand and energy of Bella, whose arm brushed the cloth as she picked up the shoes and announced, "It's now or never."

Brent offered a word of support. "I'm here for you."

"Thanks."

"Are you going to try the shoes on outside the dressing room?"

"Actually, it feels more appropriate to put them on in the bathroom."

"The bathroom?" Brent stammers with confusion. "That doesn't make any sense. You never have worn shoes you pulled on in the bathroom."

"It does make sense. The bathroom was the reason Harry came to the store." As an afterthought, Bella mumbled to herself, "At least I think that was the reason."

Reluctantly consenting, Brent said, "Leave the door open."

Using the toilet as a chair made especially for trying on shoes, Bella carefully slid her right foot and then left into the penny loafers.

Nothing.

"Anything?"

"No." Her shoulders sunk beneath the weight of disappointment. "Maybe you're too close. Step back from the doorway."

Brent obliged without objection and then asked, "How about now?" Bella shook her head.

"Maybe you must start closer to the dressing room. You can always walk back here." Like Bella, Brent was tossing out the first thing that came to mind.

Staring at the sign directly in front of the toilet. *Roses are red, Poop is brown, Flush it down, or we'll hunt you down,* Bella slowly elevated away from the lid of the seat on the porcelain bowl. As the distance from the cover increased, the more the words blended into one word and became more difficult to read. As the message faded, the aroma of stale whiskey, body odor, and human waste became overwhelming. Bella's hand cupped her mouth and nose to defuse the smell, but it only grew in intensity. She was the source.

Awareness of her body intensified as her knees screamed with each step taken away from the bathroom. It felt as though the bone was rubbing against bone. The pressure at the base of her neck exploded like a nuclear bomb filling every chamber of her brain. Taking in air made her nearly pass out because there was no room for blood to pump into the skull. Nausea pushed upward from the core of her abdomen.

Dropping to the floor of the dressing room triggered the mirror to awaken and Bella saw who she assumed was a much younger version of Harry. A very handsome, distinguished-looking professional version of Harry.

The gentleman, exuding confidence and exhibiting a degree of arrogance, was seated behind a massive wooden desk in front of a cathedral-like stained glass window. The remainder of the room was encased in shelves and shelves of books. Some of the books were placed upright, while others were stacked sideways on top of each other. The newer the book the more likely the volume was stacked sideways. The top of the desk was buried beneath layers of papers, notebooks, and more books. The actual workspace available was little more than eighteen inches by eighteen inches through which Harry would peer out from time to time.

Without any warning, Harry's chair slid toward the window. It was only then that Bella noticed Harry was not alone. With eagle-like vision, Harry inspected the individual seated before him. Bella was mesmerized by the softness of Harry's voice and how every word flowed like a lazy river moving with purpose but doing so with grace.

"So you are here to defend your midterm paper."

The voice that responded matched the petite frame of the brunette woman. "Yes, that is correct."

"As part of your defense, do you wish to add more to the work or are you simply asking that I award you a higher grade?"

The woman casually brushed aside several strands of hair from her face and drifted forward slightly as she spoke with confidence. "I believe I covered the topic well. I have a clear thesis, which I developed well. Therefore, yes, I believe that I should receive a better grade."

Harry smiled slightly as he delivered his rebuttal to the request at hand. "You selected Robert Frost and Sylvia Plath, both who died in 1963, and proposed that these two great poets were more similar than might appear at first reading of their work."

With excitement in her voice, she interrupted Harry. "Yes, that is correct. They both shed light, in a new way, on the notion of depression and death. In fact..."

With a hand raised, Harry silenced the woman. "You selected one piece from Frost, an anomaly, I might add, to compare with an entire volume of work by Platt. You would have been better off to suggest that Frost's single poem about death does not mean he is consumed by depression, darkness, and death like Platt."

Bella found herself leaning back, struggling with her own uneasiness for the woman perched across from Harry. Harry clearly controlled the space. The tension within the room intensified as Harry continued to instruct the woman on what she should have done.

"Or assuming you want to build a case that Frost's work was influenced by depression and death, it would have been appropriate to convince your reader that the volume of Frost's work, which emphasizes life, was merely his effort to avoid death. But of course, you did neither."

The candor of the woman's response gripped Bella in the throat, and she struggled to inhale. "Harry, you're not being fair."

"Jess." The way the name passed Harry's lip informed Bella that this was no longer a professor/student relationship. There was something more unfolding here. "Jess, we've had this conversation multiple times. In public you must call me professor."

Jess rose from the chair and went around the side of the wooden desk where she pushed aside a stack of papers to make room for herself to sit. She leaned in closer to Harry. The fingers of her left hand stroked Harry's forearm. Her voice softened. "Don't you see, that's the problem? You are treating me harsher than other students to prove to yourself and anyone who might discover our relationship that you were always fair. But you're not fair!"

"Jess, none of that changes the fact that in public, you must call me professor. As for your paper..."

"If that's the case, why don't you refer to me as Ms. Brinkmann? You don't get to call me Jess in public and in private."

"Now you're being irrational. You know I don't refer to any students by their last name."

Fighting to not appear to be an immature schoolgirl who cries when frustrated, her mouth tightened, her eyes narrowed, and she delivered each word with force. "Perhaps it's time you give it a try!"

The mirror went dark.

Bella leaned against the back wall and took a deep breath. The additional oxygen filled her lungs and the ends of her fingers and toes tingled. Before she could exhale, a room illuminated by a single 60-watt light bulb appeared in the mirror. The aurora cast an eerie shadow over the full-size bed. The bed clearly had not been made as the top sheet and comforter lay in a heap in the middle of the bed.

Bella shrieked as the pile of bedding moved and a foot popped out from beneath. Then a second followed by a third and a fourth. One pair of feet was attached to hairy legs, while the other set belonged to a pair of smooth, hairless legs. At the opposite end of the bedding, two heads emerged. The comforter took flight and landed across the room. Bella was able to breathe a sigh of relief as the paisley sheets stayed in place covering the body parts she preferred not to see.

"I don't understand. Why can't I move in? In two weeks, I'll be a graduate, an alum. No one will be able to question our love for one another."

"We've covered this territory before." To accentuate his position of being right, Harry added the tagline with authority, "A number of times."

"Yes. And that territory was a month and a half ago. It's two weeks, two harmless weeks, where the faculty will be consumed with preparing for finals and justifying grades. Students will be either partying or cramming for finals. And the administration will... well, who knows what occupies their time."

"Jess." Harry turned and looked into her eyes as he brushed aside strands of brunette hair. "You said it well. It's two weeks, two harmless weeks. We have been together for nearly four years. How do you compare two weeks to waiting for four years? My love for you, our love, has survived. We can do two more weeks."

With the sheet tucked under her arms, Jess sat up and blurted out, "I'm pregnant. Harry. We're pregnant. You are going to be a dad."

Harry sucked all the air out of the room, including the electricity, as the light bulb flickered twice, while the back of his head dove deep into the pillow.

After a pregnant interlude, Harry spoke as though he was asking a routine question to a classroom filled with students. "How did this happen?"

"*Seriously?* You are going to question how?"

Without turning his head, he shifted his eyes in Jess's direction and said, "You know what I mean. We took every precaution."

"Nothing is 100%. You knew the risks."

"But after four years? Really? Now?"

"Harry, you're not suggesting I meant for this to happen, are you?" Jess's voice was filled with indecision.

"No, at least not with…"

"Don't!" She shouted the words. "Don't say it! Don't go there! You know I'd never, ever. If you say it, I promise you, Harry, you will never see me again, or your baby." When she finished her nose was centimeters from Harry's face.

"Jess, I trust you would never plan such a thing. But things can happen and before you realize where you are… well, it's too late.

She ripped the sheet off Harry and wrapped it tightly around her body, the body carrying Harry's child. She stepped back from the bed and said, "Harry, I pity you. I love you with all my heart. You swept me off my feet the moment I saw you. I knew at that moment I wanted, I needed to spend the rest of my life with you. And you alone. Since you don't seem to understand, let me tell you. I'd never allow myself to get into such a situation as you describe. As much as I love you, I love myself and this baby more. I can't be with someone who doesn't trust me unconditionally. I will not subject myself or my child, your child, to such stupidity."

"Stupidity?" Harry extended his arm in an attempt to grab her hand. "Do you know what you are saying?"

"Stupidity. One hears the truth, sees the truth, knows the truth, and still believes the lie. Stupidity! Goodbye, Harry."

Before Harry could roll off the bed, Jess was out the front door and gone.

Chapter 40

"Harry, it has come to our attention that Jess Brinkmann is with child. What do you know about this?"

The question seeped into every pour of Harry's existence as he scanned the president's plush office. Harry's eyes stopped on two portraits that were displayed next to one another. The one on the right hung slightly higher than the other. The photo on the right was of George Washington, and the one on the left was Benedict Arnold, an accomplished field general. The president of the college was fond of stating, "Those two portraits capture all of U.S. History in its entirety.

Harry knew the category into which he was cast. He knew it was over. He knew he'd never teach again. He couldn't help but wonder how? How did the President find out? It was futile to ask. Just as Washington was loyal to his troops, so was the man across the desk.

The only question now was how soon?

The answer came quickly, "By the end of the day."

"What about finals? Grades?"

"No longer your concern." It was the final nail in Harry's coffin, and it felt like the president enjoyed pounding it down.

Bella recognized the person she knew as Harry as he stumbled toward the door. The word that came forth was disgraced.

It's amazing how disgraced has a look of its own. Makeup can't hide or conceal it. Body posture is controlled by it. Shoulders slump, eyes cast downward, and feet shuffle. It's difficult to envision anything more dehumanizing than being disgraced. Few can recover from such cultural improprieties.

Chapter 41

The refrigerator box was a prized possession in the railroad yard. Harry positioned himself at the opening and pointed at his shoes. He spoke as though across from him someone held a camera recording his every word. Bella could see there was no one before him, and then his voice became clear.

"Marge, now that your feet have slid into the loafers, you've seen the story of my past. What you may not know is that the loafers were the only thing that Jess has given me.. She saw them in the window as we walked the sidewalk in Estes Park, hand in hand. It was July before the start of her senior year. Her roommate from her entire time in college covered for us with the story that the two of them were on a road trip to Colorado." With a slight laugh, he added, "Jess always felt guilty about lying and therefore demanded that part of the tale be true.

"The shoes, the moment she spotted them she pulled me to the window and with her nose pressed to the glass said, "Harry, those shoes scream, Professor Harry. You have to get them. I have two pennies, one for each shoe.

"As you can see and have witnessed since you opened the Rerun Thrift Store, I bought the shoes and Jess slipped the pennies into each loafer. I promised her I'd proudly wear the shoes until the day I die. Obviously, with your feet in the loafers, I no longer take in breath. Funny how Jess's freshman paper was correct. Robert Frost knew something about death and depression, and life.

"The loafers, my dear friend. Jess always said that pontification to me was what masturbation is to other men. Please forgive me. The loafers. I have worn them every day since she left, and I carried those two priceless pennies with every step I took. I tracked down her college roommate and learned I have a daughter, Sylvia. Unfortunately, that's all she would tell me. Marge, I want you to find my daughter Sylvia. I have a priceless gift to share with her. For your efforts, you will keep $50,000 dollars in order to find your own daughter and keep the doors of Rerun Thrift Store open.

"The money, you wonder, 'Where did it come from?' It's from the penny in the left loafer. It's rare and valuable. The penny, as you will discover once it's removed, is a 1958 Lincoln Wheat Cent Penny. The value is not related to it being a wheat penny. The value is the result of doubled die obverse casting. Both *In God We Trust* and **Liberty** are double-lined. It is one of the rarest pennies made.

"I digress, but I find great humor in the fact that value is not related to perfection but imperfection. It is as though the greater the error, the greater the value. I wonder if there is a lesson here to be learned. As I said, I digress. Onward.

"Jess didn't realize what she had in her pocket! The penny is worth roughly $200,000 dollars. The value is subject to the current market, whatever some rich dude is willing to pay. It could be slightly less or considerably more.

"Marge, I am indebted to you. Thank you."

Bella cautiously stepped from the dressing room wearing only one loafer and cradling the other. Before Brent could speak, she said, "I don't know where to start, but... I do know my future. I—we, if you wish to come along—have two tasks to complete. The one first, I'll complete tomorrow. The second one... well, that may take the rest of our lives."

Epilogue

"Hi, are you Sarah? Sarah Peterson?"

"I am. Well, I was Sarah Peterson, I'm now Ms. ..."

Looking past Sarah into the living room, Bella never heard the last name as she saw two kids. A boy and a girl, both close to, if not, teenagers. One was watching TV, and the other was typing on the phone.

Sarah noticed that the visitor standing on the front step was looking past her and into the comfort of her home. With a slight shift of her body, she pulled the eyes of the young woman back to her. Then she asked, "What is it you want?"

"I have a package here for Sarah Peterson."

"A package? I didn't order anything. What is it?"

"I don't know, ma'am, I'm simply here to deliver the package."

"Who is it from?"

"I don't know that either. As I said, my job is to deliver the package. Here you go." Bella pushed the box, wrapped in brown shipping paper, into the hands of Sarah and turned to leave.

"Wait," Sarah spoke as she stepped from the entrance and onto the front step. "You look familiar. Do I know you?"

"I doubt it, ma'am. I'm new to town. This is my first day on the job, and I have more deliveries to make. I need to keep moving." Bella turned and continued to walk the length of the sidewalk toward Brent's car.

Sarah shrugged her shoulders and stepped back inside and closed the door. With the box on the dining room table, she removed the brown paper to discover that the box was wrapped in bright blue wrapping paper with silver stars. Careful so as not to tear the paper, Sarah unwrapped the box again which revealed a shoe box.

Her son from the living room yelled, "Hey, Mom, what's that? What's in the box?"

"I don't know, George. I haven't opened it yet."

"What are you waiting for? Open it already."

Sarah wasn't sure why she was reluctant to lift the cover. For a moment, she thought about the young woman who delivered the package. Why did she look so familiar?

With encouragement from both her kids who were now curious to learn what was in the box, Sarah removed the cover and lifted a pair of flip-flops.

Her daughter immediately stepped back from the table as she spoke, "Oh, gross, Mom! An old pair of shoes? Throw them away."

Her son was laughing, and saying, "Someone just pranked you, Mom."

Sarah wasn't sure but she didn't think this was a prank. The flip-flops looked vaguely familiar. As she turned them over to inspect them more closely, she saw a slip of paper taped to the bottom. The note, written in perfect penmanship, read,

These belong to you! Wear them again as you did once as a little girl. May the soles enliven your soul. Your loving daughter, Bella

Questions for Discussion and Reflection

1. If you could ask Bella one question, what would you ask? Why?

2. Discuss Marge's character.

3. Which pair of shoes was most comfortable for you, and which was most disturbing? Why?

4. What is the Dressing Room and Mirror in your life? Where do you go to reflect, to encounter the soul of another and yourself? Do these spaces just happen, or are they created?

5. How would you describe Bella's soul, the essence of her existence?

6. How do you understand the essence of life?

7. Is the soul only a spiritual, religious reference, or something more?

8. Sofie says, "To hear is more important than to see. Anyone can believe who sees, but it demands true faith to only hear and still believe." How do you respond to such "wisdom"? Is it wisdom?

9. If you were to write the sequel to *The Soul of the Shoe,* what would it be about? What issues might emerge?

10. What questions do you have for the author?

I dedicate this book to all the students I have had the opportunity to work with as a teacher, a professor, a coach, a horseman, and an equine bodyworker. Paulo Freire, in *Pedagogy of the Oppressed*, wrote, "The teacher is no longer merely the-one-who-teaches, but one who is taught in dialogue with the students, who in turn while being taught also teach… People teach each other, mediated by the world, by the cognizable objects…" (61) In that moment, when such a transformation occurs, there exists the exchange and evolution of thought. Knowledge now has a purpose. A purpose to create a more just and peaceful world. A world where empathy is not merely a feeling but an action, a way of living.

I want to thank the students who welcomed me into their evolution of thought. Students from the classroom, the stable, the arena, the athletic spaces, and the pastures of daily life. Bella is a compilation of the students I was blessed to walk alongside for a brief period. Thank you!

Thank you to Michael Braun, my editor for this project and the new owner of Orange Hat Publishing. Michael went above and beyond to ensure that the message within the pages above was discernible and that the voice of each character was clear. In the spirit of Orange Hat, as started by Shannon Ishizaki, Michael will carry on and take it to new heights.

Thank you to Shannon Ishizaki for taking time during her final days at Orange Hat to work on the cover design. I truly cannot imagine where I'd be as an author without her guidance and support over the years.

The cover picture was designed and painted by Julie Schweiss. Julie is a gifted and talented Minnesota artist who, stepping aside from the family business, is once again following her passion. For this we are all blessed as we can enjoy her artwork. Thank you for painting the cover picture and for inviting me to be a part of your new studio, Julie Schweiss Studio in Hector, MN.

Thank you to Anikka Knick, Miranda Stueckrath, and Tanya Brossand for reading early drafts and providing insightful and constructive comments and questions.

As always, thank you to my wife, Tammie Haven Knick, for her willingness to listen as I struggled with various sections of the book and for her endless support and encouragement.

Finally, although Bella doesn't encounter a real live horse in the story, horses are a critical component to the success of writing this book. Our horses, all five of them, each in their own way, provided me with the opportunity to keep one boot planted in reality and another in a world of imagination.

If you enjoyed this book, I invite you to check out my other books.

Kingdom of Collectible Treasures
The Mist of Salvation
Horses In Heaven
In The Right Place
Fall on Me

Milton Keynes UK
Ingram Content Group UK Ltd.
UKHW040142301024
450367UK00022BA/161